Carlos the Cloud

and other stories

ALSO BY JIM GOLD

Fiction

Songs and Stories for Open Ears

Mad Shoes:
From Bronx violinist to Bulgarian folk dancer

Handfuls of Air: Fights of Fresh Air Fantasy

Zany! A Father-Son Odyssey

Non-Fiction

A New Leaf (5 volumes)

A New Leaf: Adventures in the Creative Life

A Treasury of International Folk Dances:
A Step-by-Step Guide Choreographed by Jim Gold

Carlos the Cloud

and other stories

JIM GOLD

Full Court Press
Englewood Cliffs, New Jersey

First Edition

Copyright © 2020 by Jim Gold

Published in the United States of America
by Full Court Press, 601 Palisade Avenue,
Englewood Cliffs, NJ 07632
fullcourtpress.com

Print ISBN 978-1-946989-69-7
Ebook ISBN 978-1-946989-70-3
Library of Congress Control Nunber: 2020909385

Editing and book design by Barry Sheinkopf

To Bernice

*For all the years
of love and learning*

TABLE OF CONTENTS

Carlos the Cloud

*E*VERY MORNING AT DAWN, Father Sun dressed Carlos the Cloud in his moisture suit and sent him floating across the Spanish sky. All day long Carlos played with his black and white cloud buddies as they drifted between Granada and Cordoba. Every evening at dusk, Carlos settled above an olive tree in Jaen province. There he rested, to enjoy the stars shining above him.

When dawn arrived, he drank his moisture breakfast, marveled at his bulging nebulous muscles, proudly showed them off to the other clouds, then burst. Rain fell. The Spanish flowers and trees enjoyed a good drink.

Next day, Carlos floated up to Father Sun. Patting his new nebulae, he said, "I like raining. The flowers are smiling. Earth likes me. Trees, rivers, shade, and humans appreciate what I do. I want to rain on them again. When can I do it again?"

"When you're full," Father Sun answered.

Carlos continued playing and the centuries passed.

One day, a storm blew him to Seattle. Floating above the

Microsoft building, he rained on a worker. The man looked up. Shaking his finger at Carlos, he shouted, "You stupid cloud! Soon you'll be nothing but a drop. You dumped on me. But that's no reason to be proud of your aim, or happy you scored. Earth is warming, drying up. You'll soon be an afterthought, a nothing, a transient moment in the universe." His face reddened with rage before he fell to his knees, kissed the ground, and began to cry, "Good-bye Earth. Global warming will kill us all. Soon I'll be an afterthought, too, unnoticed and forgotten."

Carlos wanted to hear more of this strange man's weather forecast, but a gust of wind blew him to Alaska. Weeks later, hovering above a San Diego beach, he still thought about the stinging words of the frightened Microsoft man. For the first time in his life, Carlos felt dissatisfied.

He consulted with his father. "Does my cloud burst make me transient?" he asked. "Why grow if I end up empty?" Surprised by his sudden questions, he paused to consider their (philosophical) depth. "Am I really a nothing in cloud form?"

"Well," answered Father Sun, "transience *is* a problem for clouds. In fact, it's a problem for everything and everyone. It makes them sad. (Transience is sad.) But watering the soil, helping trees and flowers grow, filling empty rivers, and bringing drinks to thirsty people helps heal the world." Father Sun sent a ray of sunshine to a poor family beneath him. "Making others happy is a good thing."

"That's nice to know, Father. But it doesn't make me feel any better. I'll still end up empty, a blank wisp of nothing."

Carlos was about to cry when he saw his father's mood changing. The kindly, wise patron of the arts and ruler of the sky began to increase his heat. The fire of his eye burned molten hot. Hammered by the whiny complaints of his spoiled, unappreciative cloud, he shook his giant finger and roared, "You dumb, short-sighted, arrogant snot! Your lack of gratitude *disgusts* me. Keep this up, and you'll never make Storm Category."

Carlos winced. He shrank to the size of a molecule.

When Father Sun saw his pain, he softened. "Stop shriveling, Carlos. Keep this up, and soon you'll be just an element. Don't worry. I won't hurt you. No need to fear *criticism*. I *love* you. Think about it like this. When flowers and trees grow, you grow as well. You're a team working together. Without your water the others can't exist. And without the others, you have no purpose. Think of your rain as a blessing. As you rain and shrink, the plants and trees grow. And in the process, you grow in wisdom."

"Who cares about wisdom?" Carlos whined. "Who cares about plants, trees, and rivers. I don't want to fill and empty all day. I want muscles. I want to be big and strong."

"Sure you do. Every cloud wants to be big and strong. And you will become that."

"Great!"

"But there are limits."

"For me? I thought I was your favorite cloud."

"Certainly, you are one of my favorites. But there are limits for me."

"Do you have limits?"

"Yes, for me, too. Everyone has limits."

"Really? How sad."

"No, no. Not completely sad. True, everyone has limits. But no one knows what they are."

"Do *you* know?"

"No. Or, at least I'm not telling you about them. However, many people in this world believe I *do* know. Let them think what they like." Father Sun paused to let his lesson sink in. "But," he continued, "everyone and everything has limits. And aside from the basics—like the life and death cycle—no one knows what their limitations *are*."

"Can I still grow as big and strong as I want?"

"You'll grow until you burst. That's the life of a cloud."

"But I want muscles!"

His father sighed in frustration. "I can see you're still young and stupid." Searching for an example, he looked down at Earth, and pointed to a crew of men on Pearl Street loading furniture into a truck. "Those guys down there are just like you. Fill and empty, load and unload, that's their job. When they're finished, they go home from work. And after they put in many years of service, *I* call them home. They rest here awhile. Then, I send them down again to do another job."

"You mean they die?"

"In a sense."

"Is that what filling and emptying is?"

"You're a smart cloud. Figure it out."

Scratching the moisture on his belly, Carlos thought about transitions. Finally, he asked, "Can raining my waters ever reward me?"

Father smiled. "Of course. Raining unburdens you, makes you light and free. After you give it all away, you can float free and easy through the sky. I'd call that a refreshment. Tasty, too."

Carlos hovered in place for several hours. "Father, where were *you* last night?" he finally asked.

"I was asleep."

"Did you die?"

"Of course. I do that every night."

"Is it sad?"

"It can be, but only for a while. I need my rest, so I can travel and expand. But I always come back the next day."

"Dying must be easy for you. You're an old man."

"You can die at any age, Carlos. It can be painful, but the benefits of travel and expansion make it easier."

"Where do you go?"

"Mostly to Cycle Rest Homes."

"What are they?"

"A chain of homes in quiet corners of the universe. The first home for Neolithic hungers was started during the Paleolithic period by Nan See, a local female Neanderthal entrepreneur. When her first client, Baboosh, returned to Earth rested and energized, other hunters started using her Cycle Rest home services as well. Due to the growth of mammoth hunts in what is now called Siberia, Cycle Rest Homes expanded. Today there are hundreds throughout the universe."

Father Sun shone a few hours on Argentina, then continued. "I use them all the time. It takes energy to create light, so I need lots of breaks. After a few hours resting in my Home, I feel renewed. Then I come out to create a dawn."

"That's weird."

"Yes, dying is weird, but it works. Just like you can't wake up unless you sleep, and you can't be reborn unless you die. Remember what Baboosh said after his first mammoth hunt: 'Gogoo possimus porticantius lodos.' (If you want to live, you have to die.)"

"Is that what expansion is all about?"

"Yes. Emptying, then filling. It's the only way to go."

Carlos floated as he considered this. Finally, with a burst of enthusiasm, he cried, "I want to expand, too. I want to accumulate. I want to become the biggest cloud in the sky!"

"That's a healthy attitude, Carlos, although a tad competitive. But every cloud wants to get bigger and stronger, to expand and float across the sky."

"That's for me!"

"Okay, but when you rain and vanish, will you still be disappointed? Will you still complain?"

"I think I can take it."

"Good. Who knows—you may even *become* the biggest cloud in the sky. But rather than dwell on size, better to think about the glorious healing water you will give others. That's the most important part of cloud life. Now go play with your friends."

"Thank you, Father."

And Carlos floated across the Spanish sky.

Swamp Disorder

STAN AND MOLLY WERE LOVERS of a premier order. Their roars, cries, laughter, and general bedroom antics were the talk of the neighborhood. People heard their joyous screams miles away and often called the police or fire department when their howls of delight and rapture became too cacophonous.

"A noisy bunch," complained Lesley Parsnip, their next-door neighbor.

"Shut them up!" grumbled Gaylord McCullough, the neighbor across the street. "We can't sleep a wink."

"I wish they'd watch TV," said their itinerant mailman, Peepod Poley.

Stan and Molly burnt up the neighborhood with their love cries, causing friction, jealousy, and hatred among neighbors and destroying the very fabric of society.

One day, Stan read an ad in the *New York Scenes*:

"Are you looking for happiness, satisfaction, and inner

peace? Does your stomach turn every time you go to work? Do you detest your home and hate your neighbors? If you suffer from these debilitating conditions, come to Henry's Place!

"We'll give you a cool beer, tasty pretzels, and a glimpse of the afterlife. Some people say we're Heaven on Earth. We say we're Earth in Heaven. Either way, you'll want to experience our joy connection for yourself.

"We're located on Pharaoh Island, just across the causeway. To reach us, drive down Route 16, pass the Great Swamp on your right, and see our blue sign straight ahead."

Stan put down his morning coffee. "Read this," he said, looking up at Molly. "Sounds good. Let's go this afternoon."

Molly turned from her soup bowl, picked up her reading glasses, and read the ad. "I love you, Stan," she crooned. "I'll do anything to make you happy. But frankly, this Henry's Place sounds stupid. What's this happiness, bliss, and higher powers stuff? Who believes in that? Sounds like whitewash from the sixties."

"Thank you, dear. Always trying to please me! You're so *selfless*. I don't think you even have an ego, but if you do, it must be the size of a shoe."

"I can't go now," Molly continued. "I'm seeing my therapist. But still, having beer and pretzels might be a fun way to celebrate our love. How about Sunday?"

"I thought you were working on spontaneity in your sessions. How about today?" Stan stamped his foot to emphasize the point. "This is practice time. How about right now?"

Molly reconsidered. "Okay. Okay," she said, loving the wild excitement in Stan's eyes. "Dr. Abramowitz can wait. Let's do it."

They climbed into their Mercedes. Stan turned on the ignition and the car sputtered to life. Snippets of *Götterdammerung* sounded through the back-door speakers.

They headed for Route 16, passing red brick houses, cattle farms, and a Congregationalist graveyard.

Soon, a forest of maples lined with hydrangea beds framed their path. When they turned onto Route 16, a sudden wild gust of wind from the west drove the scattered clouds across the sky with jack-booted speed. The sun broke through.

They passed Murphy's Drug and Food Mart and came to an open farmland field. A wide-open road and two miles of nothingness stood before them. They drove on, and suddenly the Great Swamp appeared.

"Look, there's the Great Swamp," shouted Stan.

"Where?"

"On our right."

Molly looked. "That's our left."

"Right."

"Left," she countered.

"Can't we agree on anything this morning?" Stan grunted. "That's our right."

"You're wrong. That's our left." Molly rolled up her window and pouted. "Let's call Dr. Abramowitz. He'll know."

"You don't have to consult your therapist for *everything*. It's on the right. No doubt about it."

Molly sighed, then softened. "Okay, you win. What's the difference? Right or left, who cares? I'm an up-and-down person, anyway. Stop the car. I want to check out this swamp."

"Molly, don't you want to spend some real time at Henry's Place? It's only a *swamp*. Check it from the car."

"You must be kidding. I never pass up a swamp opportunity. You know me better than that. I *must* see it!"

Stan pulled the car to the side of the road. When they got out, he gazed at the sky. Molly stared at the swamp, totally transfixed. "This is a *swamp*!" she said in disgust. "I've rarely seen one like it. I can't *stand* it. It must be *eradicated*. I *hate* swamps! *All* swamps!"

"Oh, let this one go, Molly. We'll never get to Henry's once you start."

"No! There's no stopping me, Stan. I must. It's my calling. The call of the Hebrew prophets was mild compared to this. My calling comes directly from God. We cannot move another inch until this entire mess is *cleaned up*!"

"But—but it will ruin our day. We'll never make it to Henry's Place."

"The hell with Henry's Place. I'm on fire! I don't care a damn about Henry's Place. I want to improve the environment and create world peace!"

Stan pulled back, reflected a moment. "Well, all right," he said, his voice low in resignation. "It doesn't look *that* big. Let's give it a try."

"Good. Thank you, dear, for being so understanding. The world will be a better place after we clean this up."

They opened the trunk, took out two shovels, a pair of scissors, and three Band-Aids, and started clearing out the Great Swamp.

"This shouldn't take us more than a day or two," said Molly cheerily.

"I hope you're right, but I think it'll take at least a week. We'll see. Whatever it takes, do you still want to go to Henry's Place when we're finished?"

"Of *course*, dear. Isn't that why we came in the first place? I never break a commitment, although sometimes there are delays."

"Swamp cleaning can do that."

FOUR WEEKS LATER, STAN SAID, "This is huge. We'll never get it cleaned up by ourselves. We need help."

Molly sat on a log, wiping the sweat off her forehead. "Sadly, I have to agree," she murmured in a low voice heavy with exhaustion.

"I'm glad you do," Stan said. "I know a few swamp experts. They've been cleaning out bogs for years—peat, sycamore splinters, soda cans, plastic bottles, everything. I ran into them on a demolition job. Want me to give them a call?"

"I'm ready," Molly sighed. "I'm on the verge of defeat."

"Defeat? Molly, I'm surprised at you. Never give up! But we do need some help."

He searched the contacts in his cell phone. "Ah, here it

is!" He punched in the number. "These guys can clean anything."

After a couple of rings, he heard a voice. "Hello. Gus Weed here, president of Swamp Therapies. What can I do for you?"

"Hello, Gus. This is your old friend, Stan."

"Who's Stan?"

"We met at the Tree Stump Removal Convention in Atlantic City. Do you remember?"

A long silence. "You're the rodent salesman."

"No, that was another Stan. I'm the walnut guy."

"Oh, yeah, the one with the nut hat."

"Right."

"Okay. What's up?"

"My wife and I are here in the Great Swamp. We're trying to clean it up, but having a helluva time and not much success. We need some help."

"You mean Long Bog Swamp?"

"No, the Great Swamp. The one next to Long Bog."

"Oh, yeah, the one with milk cartons." Gus turned in his swivel chair. "Hey, Larry, take over the office. I'm on a road call." He returned to the phone. "Okay, Mr. Stan. No problem. Be there in under an hour."

Gus put on his green "Make New Jersey Great" hat, rose from his desk, grabbed a tuna sandwich from the refrigerator, and hopped into his Swamp Truck.

WHEN HE REACHED THE SWAMP SITE, Molly was sitting on a log, crying. Stan stood beside her, helplessly waving a handkerchief.

Gus opened the back of his truck and pulled out his Swamp Repair Kit. He ambled over to Molly, patted her head, and sat down next to her. "There, there, dear client," he said in a low, soothing voice. "Lie back. Rest. Relax. Feel the leg support beneath you. Let the branches be your pillow. Easy. Relax. No worries. Gus is here."

"I cleaned, cleaned, cleaned," she bawled. "And nothing *happened*! No matter how many roots and branches I pulled out, I kept finding more."

"That's the nature of a swamp," Gus commiserated.

"I hate the flies and rats. I hate them all!" Molly sat up in terror. "And the bog never ends."

"I understand. Relax . . . relax." Gus guided her back to prone position and looked in her eyes. "But there is good news."

"Oh?"

"Yes. Bogs can make you feel good. They can even create health."

"They can?" Molly wiped away a tear.

"Yes, bogs are the way to go. Most folks around here live in or near a bog. They pay good money to do so. Living near or, even better, *in* a bog is your first step to salvation."

Molly stopped crying. "What are you talking about?"

"It's a matter of perspective. Take the expression 'bogged down.' This expression was introduced by a Dutch anthro-medievalist in 1642. One day, a dike leaked and flooded his farm with sea water. After that he learned how walk with mud on his boots, lifting each foot high as he carried that extra weight. Such lifting built not only his leg muscles, but his character, inner strength, and fortitude as well. Once you can handle a bog, dealing with swamp disorder is easy. Our company has created a bog training manual and our Bog-and-Swamp doctoral program is the best in the nation."

All Molly could do now was utter a soft, lame "Are you crazy?"

"Now, my dear," Gus continued, "I can see from the pimples on your legs that you have worshipped swamps for many years. And that is good. But because you are so short, your diminished stature has caused you to embrace the worship of lower things. But, short or tall, it's always better to aim higher. That's what Swamp Therapy is all about. We lift you out of the swamp, put you on dry land, and, once stabilized, lift your mental processes to a higher plane."

Molly blinked her eyes, as a mix of disbelief and wonder passed through them.

"In the beginning," Gus continued, "focusing on a toad or tree stump is considered a step up. But once the cells in your brain start the leavening process, your skills slowly increase and move even higher."

Gus took Molly by the hand, pulled her to her feet. He pointed to the branch of a willow tree about one hundred feet away. "For today," he said, "the best way to raise your perception will be to sit up there."

Molly stretched her arms. "I don't think I can do it, Gus. It's hard for me to climb."

"Of course," he answered. "That's why you're in the

swamp."

He guided her across sand, twigs, and wet leaves. "You can do it," he assured her. "It's not easy to rise. But others have done it. And I know you can, too."

Stan stood by his car, pleased with the progress of the process. "You sure know your stuff. I know a good communicator when I see one."

Gus nodded. "Communication is good," he said, looking Stan straight in the eye. "But watch out for those who force it on you. Such pressure can kill originality. Imagination thrives on freedom. That's why Swamp Therapy works so well. We use our Swamper vacuum cleaner to suck out blockage and clear the path of creativity. It takes about ten minutes to vacuum a mental mess. Our prices beat any therapist. You may want to pick one up. When we get to our office, speak to my partners."

"Where's your office?"

"Just down the road. Next to Henry's Place."

"Henry's Place? When we started out a month ago, that's where we wanted to go! But we were sidetracked by the Swamp."

"Many are."

"My wife insisted on cleaning it up. She wouldn't leave until the job was done."

"An impossible task."

"Perfection is her mission."

"I understand her sad situation. So many want perfection. But those who achieve it never get out alive."

Molly, now awake and focused, listening intently.

"Really?"

"Yes." Gus took her hand and looked deeply into her eyes. "The insistence on perfection creates utopia, and utopia is death."

"I thought utopia was heaven."

"Same thing."

Molly seemed puzzled. "Then is Henry's Place really a graveyard?" she asked.

"You could call it that."

"But isn't it beautiful, peaceful, serene?"

"It is."

Stan stepped forward. "Maybe this is the wrong time to visit. We're not ready for Henry's Place. Let's turn around and go home. We're still young."

Gus said, "Age is no problem. Folks visit us anytime. We accept all guests."

Stan felt disappointed. Molly was crushed. "All my life, I wanted to clean things up, fix the swamp, make a perfect world."

"Improving things is good."

"But you say the end result of perfection is a visit to Henry's Place."

"Yes. It is the insistence on perfection that kills."

"I'm an insistent person."

"Yes, you are. Not a bad thing."

"But I don't want to die."

"No reason for that."

Stan looked at Molly. Molly looked at Stan. Both looked at Gus. "We want to go home," they said in one voice.

"You mean back to the swamp?"

Wistfully, the couple nodded.

"Back to endless cleaning?"

"Yes," Stan answered. "And I want to start clarinet lessons."

"Then you'll visit Henry's Place sometime in the future?"

"Okay."

Gus reached into his pocket, took out his departure hat, and stretched his arms to the sky.

"Okay, I'm leaving. We're finished for now. Life is a swamp. If you want to get out of it, you're dead."

Gus climbed into his Swamp Truck, started the motor.

"See you soon!" he said, and sped off.

Laughing Turnip

TOM LEGUME HAD A VEGETABLE GARDEN in his backyard where he planted rows of tomatoes, corns, potatoes, Swiss chard, carrots, cucumbers, and turnips.

At the end of the summer, he started picking his vegetables, filling baskets with tomatoes, corn, potatoes, Swiss chard, carrots, cucumbers . . . and turnips.

"Ha, ha, ha!"

Tom looked around. Who was laughing? No one else was in the garden. He bent to pick some more.

"Ha, ha, ha!"

"*Who's that*?" He looked in his basket.

"Ha, ha, ha!"

It was the turnip! Really?

Tom had never heard a laughing turnip before. He shook his head in wonder.

But soon his confusion turned into an idea. His mother and father needed cash to open a dry-cleaning business. No one had ever heard of a laughing turnip. With proper promotion, this vegetable could make lots of money.

The next day, Tom took the turnip to Pathmark, where he laid it beside his purchases at the checkout counter. When the turnip laughed, the checkout man eyed Tom. "Young man, are you laughing at me?"

"No, sir," answered Tom. "It's my turnip."

"You think I'm stupid?"

"No, no. There it is on the counter." Tom pointed to the dormant vegetable. The turnip laughed.

"Watch out, kid. Anyone laughs at me gets smacked in the face."

"It's not me. It's my—"

When the turnip laughed again, the checkout man grabbed a broom. "Get out!" he shouted, swinging the broom. Tom grabbed his turnip and ran out the door.

Next he went to the hardware store. The turnip laughed again. "Sorry," Tom apologized to the manager. "It's my turnip."

"Just pay for the hammer," the manager sighed. "Why do I get all the nutcases?"

Tom began to doubt himself as left the store. "Who will believe me? What can I do with my turnip?"

He walked several miles in deep thought. Suddenly, he cried, "*TV stations*! *They'll* believe me!"

He visited the local WBBB-TV station and showed his turnip to the director. The director called management. Management loved it! Rubbing his hands with glee, the director said, "No other station has one. Our ratings will soar!"

Then the head of sales added, "We can't put a naked turnip on TV. Let's dress him up."

They dressed the turnip in a shirt, tie, jacket, pressed pants, and polished black shoes. After that, the vegetable looked quite handsome. Management decided to give him his own talk show.

The new show, called "Turnip Time," opened in December in a prime-time spot. Audiences loved the Laughing Turnip. Holiday sales increased after he answered all their questions with a laugh. As his speaking ability improved, he expanded the breadth and depth of his answers, commenting on politics, human relations, gender marriage, space travel, and the weather. He punctuated every sentence with a healthy chortle.

Management then changed his name to Ted Turnip.

Years passed. Much of the country became vegetarian. Ted made so much money he soon gave up his talk show and bought the TV station, a farm, and a garden in the country—and then he gave up laughing altogether.

At that point, Ted Turnip didn't need Tom Legume anymore. He gave him twenty-one dollars for his service as a talent scout and told him to kiss off.

Meanwhile, Tom's parents' dry-cleaning business was nearly bankrupt. But Tom wouldn't quit. The following spring, he planted another garden. *Fourteen* laughing turnips came up. Using one of them as a talk-show host and the others as reporters, actors, and ad reps, he started his own TV station.

After his network raked in its first million, he saved his parents' business with a quick infusion of cash.

When Ted Turnip heard about Tom's new success, vegetable jealousy drained the vital juices from his green heart, and soon, like any other dried vegetable, he shriveled up and died.

Today, Ted is planted in the Vegetable Graveyard owned by none other than the entrepreneur Tom Legume. The Graveyard recently raised its entrance fee to ten dollars per lettuce head—all tax deductible.

The Larry John Story

T HE APPEARANCE OF LARRY JOHN, the biblical schizophrenic also known and John and Larry, created a sen-
sation in the biblical world. John—or was it Larry?—was
the only schizophrenic to climb Mount Sinai with Moses and
try stamping out the burning bush.

In retribution, biblical writers eradicated him. Not a
mention of his name in the *Torah*, nothing in the *Pentateuch*,
not an iota of Greek print in the *Septuagint*, and not even a
comma in the *Hamesh Hamisha*.

Scholars claim that in the end, Aaron carried off the
Larry part . . . or was it John?

A Cloudy Day

ONE MORNING, MAX WOKE UP, stretched his lanky body, dropped to the floor for three yoga salutes to the sun, and headed downstairs to the kitchen for a cup of his Colombian coffee.

He looked through the window into his backyard garden. Freshly planted vegetables sprouted beneath a gray, forbidding sky.

Another cloudy day.

He sat down, sipped his stimulant, and opened his morning philosophy reading from the *Book of Chai*.

Twenty minutes later, he looked out the window again. Still cloudy.

Clouds made Max anxious. While a single cloud merely predicted a miserable day, multiple clouds signified the collapse of the world.

He turned to his muse, Helen. "How should I handle these sad cosmic vapors?" he asked. "Watch them drift by?

Or better to dive into their mist and seize their creative powers?"

Helen listened in silence.

After an hour of waiting, Max decided to phone his neighbor, Sarah Blondshein.

After six rings, Sarah answered. "Yeees?"

"I'm sinking into misery," Max complained. "What should I do?"

"Keep sinking, and see what happens," Sarah answered. Then she hung up.

Max stroked the smooth surface of his phone as he considered her advice.

Finally, his muse spoke up. "Sarah's right. Sinking is best. Dive straight in." Helen moved closer to his ear, gently whispering encouragement directly into his cochlea and semicircular canals. "You'll be surprised at the results. Run down the street. Play your flute. Pluck a guitar string. Move! It really doesn't matter what you do, as long as you do *something*."

Max leaned on the refrigerator, balanced on one leg, and took another sip of coffee. "I like your approach, Helen. Diving into the maelstrom of mist won't make me feel any worse. And that's already a step upward."

"I'm glad you agree." Helen drifted toward the faucet. "But the emergence of your cloudy vision three days in a row means it's time for your annual psychiatric checkup."

Max raised his right finger. "Aha, you're right. You had recommended I see Dr. Woe. Sitting in his woe-chair and hearing him snore during my eight sessions relaxed me. But last year he retired. Anyone else you can recommend?"

"Dr. Ariu Philingut is excellent. He is trained in dream therapy at Baton University in Australia. He is also an excellent drummer, plays on weekends with the band Mixed Cookies. He's upbeat, off-beat, and the happiest psychiatrist I know. Make an appointment with him for a feelings checkup. But it's important to remember his twenty-three-ring phone rule, so when you call, don't hang up."

Max's eyes shone with new hope. Help was on the way. "I'm diving in right now!" he exclaimed. With trembling fingers, he punched in the number on his iPhone.

Dr. Philingut's phone rang one, two, three times . . . four, five, six . . . Max wondered, was the doctor in? Seven, eight . . . then Max remembered the rule, and hung on . . . Nine, ten, eleven, twelve . . . his first twinge of doubt emerged. Twelve, thirteen, fourteen . . . maybe the doctor really isn't there . . . fifteen, sixteen, seventeen. I'm starting to get angry. If this keeps up, I'll try figuring it out myself? . . . Eighteen, nineteen, twenty . . . I'm hanging up. Twenty-one, twenty-two. This is hopeless! Twenty-three—

"Hello? Dr. Philingut here. Feeling good this morning?"

The doctor's calm and joyful voice brought Max immediate relief. His pulse slowed, his muscles relaxed. He felt better. Now he understood the reason for the doctor's twenty-three-times rule, and realized the wisdom behind it. Dr. Philingut knew that waiting through a long series of rings created *confidence*. Most of his patients only called when they felt panic. By the seventh ring, those who didn't hang up slowly gave up hope of ever reaching the doctor. By the tenth, they had abandoned it completely. In this hopeless state, they realized they'd have to handle their problems by themselves. This independence gave birth to greater confidence and patience. By the fourteenth ring, most of his patients felt better, and hung up.

They also saved money, since Dr. Philingut charged half his fee for unanswered calls.

"Can humor lift depression and chase clouds away?" Max asked.

"Of course," the doctor answered in a jovial voice. "Your answer is found in the word 'humor' itself. What is 'humor' but 'you more.' Or more of *you*! The more of you you put in, the better the outcome, and thus, the better your depression."

". . . You mean, if I know myself better, I'll be even more depressed?"

"Precisely. More is better. Most is best. Eventually, your depression squeezes you so tightly you can't stand it anymore. At that point, it will burst."

"*Burst*? Burst into *what*?"

"Why, into *song*, of course. The song of freedom! The same with terror, panic, claustrophobia, and many other maladies. Just squeeze them until they burst. Then they disappear. Their residue is freedom."

Max listened in wonder, as the doctor continued, "The opposite of squeezing is expansion. That's why growth and collapse, development and decay, are all in one family."

"Aha! Thank you, Doctor," Max said. "I feel worse already."

"Good. The worse you feel today, the better you'll feel tomorrow."

Max hung up. "Now *I'm* feeling good," he said. He smiled to himself. "They don't call him Dr. Philingut for nothing."

Then Max went for a walk.

John in Never-Always Land

JOHN'S ARTERIES COULD HARDLY HOLD the massive quantities of misery flowing through them. Lost and alone, with no purpose or meaning to his life, he sat in his bathtub in Riverdale, New York, waiting for the resurrection.

Suddenly, the good angel Bartholowette descended. "Dear John," she cooed, waving her celestial hand above his head, "do not despair. Rebirth is in sight. My company, Flow Right, makes resurrection pills you can buy at your local pharmacy. They'll cure you! Get thee to a pharmacy!"

She floated out the window and hopped a shuttle to Venus.

John remained in his tub, baffled but hopeful. Soon he rose, tied a towel round his waist, put on his pants, shoes, and shirt, and headed for the local Riverdale CVS.

The pharmacist greeted him at the counter. "How are you, my young wire?" he asked. "What would you like?"

"I need a resurrection pill."

"Flow Right makes an excellent product."

"Yes, please give me Flow Right."

"Capsule or liquid form?"

"Capsule. Give them to me immediately!"

"Well, well, you *are* angry this morning." The pharmacist reached to the shelf and took down a jar of Flow Right Resurrection. He read the label, "*Warning: Do not open. Swallow complete bottle. Total cure will follow.*"

He handed John the bottle. "I've seen it work."

"But swallowing the bottle will kill me."

"Precisely."

"Yeah, but—but I don't want to *die*."

"Without death, one cannot be resurrected."

John placed the bottle on his tongue, swished it around in his mouth, swallowed it in one gulp, and dropped dead.

Sirens wailed. An ambulance rushed to the pharmacy.

"What is your graveyard preference?" asked a kindly attendant in a white suit.

"We don't *do* resurrection in New York," the pharmacist responded. "Take him across the bridge to Jersey. They'll take care of him."

Crankyville

W HEN THE SUN ROSE IN CRANKYVILLE, locals cried. As it climbed higher into the clear blue sky, warming the good earth, they sat in their backyards wailing. At dinners that included delicious steaks, rich wines, and succulent desserts, they moaned.

Crankyville residents were not a happy lot.

Then one day, after 9.3 months of incubation, Lawrence and Emily Cranky gave birth to the Sam child. "He is a strange creature," noted Mrs. Cranky. "See how his eyes shine?" Sure enough, when Sam saw the sun rise, his eyes lit up and he crawled around his crib, singing. Noon was giggling time; evenings, he breast-fed with happy gurgles.

Puzzled and on the verge of outrage, Mrs. Cranky shook her head. "Such a strange child," she lamented. "What is wrong with him?"

"We can't have him go around *smiling* all day," declared Mr. Cranky, slamming his fist on the table. "What will the neighbors think? Let's bring him to Leslie Pissencure, the sad therapist."

"You're right, Lawrence. It's a down day in Crankyville when you see a child smile. And our own son! How embarrassing! It's too much to bear." She broke down in a grin.

Mr. Cranky took her hand. "Don't worry, dear," he assured her. "Dr. Pissencure is excellent. She'll fix our Sam so he never smiles again."

"You're wonderful," sighed Mrs. Cranky. "What would I do without you? . . . If there is one thing I can't *stand*, it's a happy child."

The Crankies took Sam to the Teary Pavilion of Lachrymose Hospital, which specialized in cases of public happiness. Dr. Pissencure gave the boy misery miracle drugs and depressive talk therapy for two years. But even those powerful modern techniques couldn't stop the baby from gurgling, smiling at the staff, and rocking with excitement when the sun came up. Soon, Dr. Pissencure gave up.

"He is a danger to the community," said the hospital's chief surgeon. "If he keeps laughing, we'll all be out of business. We need something drastic, like the scalding rag. We'll dip it in boiling oil and wipe that smile off his face."

They wiped Sam's face with the rag. But he kept smiling. Then he laughed.

At that moment, the hospital fell down.

Jack and Jill
and the Big Bad Wolf

ONCE UPON A TIME THERE WAS A BOY named Jack, a pretty average eleven-year-old, except he was thirteen feet tall. One other thing: his left foot was a size thirteen, but his right was six miles long.

When he strolled across the country, his right foot demolished entire cities and towns. He went west from New York, heading for California. He started on his left foot, and *clump!* His right foot landed on Cleveland. That was the end of Cleveland. Then St. Louis: Clump! Albuquerque: Clump!

Finally, he reached the battered, flattened, and former city of San Francisco and took a walk on the beach.

There he met an eleven-year-old girl with braids named Jill. Her left hand looked average, but her right was six miles long. And she never walked, just skidded.

Jack liked her immediately. "Let's be friends," he said.

She held out her right hand. "Sure," she said. "Shake on it."

"Hold on," he warned. "Friendship takes time."

They swam in the ocean and frolicked on the beach for two years. Then they got a phone call from the mayor of Santa Fe. The Big Bad Wolf had retired from the book he lived in and had taken up residence in the Sandia Mountains. Every Wednesday at midnight, he rolled into Santa Fe for a human snack and ate up a

person or two. The Santa Fe population was dwindling. At first, residents had merely been frightened, but with real estate values falling *and* the threat of becoming the wolf's midnight supper, they were terrified.

"Come on over, Jack!" the mayor pleaded. "Bring Jill, too. We need all the help we can get."

Having read in the *San Francisco Kabbalah Beach* that every mitzvah creates an angel, Jack and Jill agreed to help. Holding hands, they clump-skidded towards Santa Fe.

Wednesday night found them waiting for the Big Bad Wolf in the town plaza. Sure enough, at midnight he arrived. Huge and hairy, his gray coat streaked with black, his mouth was salivating as he contemplated his upcoming midnight snack.

Jill walked right up to him. The Big Bad Wolf bared his teeth and growled ferociously.

Jill shook her head. "Bad manners," she said. "That is not the way a civilized person greets somebody. A civilized person shakes hands."

The wolf, puzzled by this sudden identity problem, said, "I—I don't have a hand."

"A foot will do," said Jill. "Or a paw."

The wolf put out his paw. Jill shook it with her six-mile hand, and that was the end of the Big Bad Wolf.

Thereafter, Jack and Jill became local Santa Fe heroes. They decided to settle in Santa Fe and open a vegetarian restaurant.

Burt's Brain

WHAT'S IN THE DUELING HEMISPHERES of Burt's brain? Yesterday, I examined it. Here's what I found:

Fires are burning in Burt's brain. Mostly in the right side. Giant fires, thousands of feet tall. Flames are shooting into the sky, incinerating planets and galaxies—even the Milky Way.

On Burt's left side, in the other hemisphere, lies a great lake filled with pure, clear water. Peaceful and calm, it sits in silence, absorbing the sun.

One day, one of the fires in Burt's brain had an idea. "I'm dynamic, creative, adventurous, and smart," it boasted. "I like to try new things." Considering his options, fire lowered his flame. "My finances are zero. I hate penury. I need some money." Then he crackled, "How should I get it? Borrowing is so boring." He thought a moment. "I know. I'll steal it! That's exciting, especially if I don't get caught. First, I'll steal a dollar. I'll use it to buy a slice of pizza. After that,

I'll steal ten dollars, then twenty, thirty, a hundred! Soon I'll be the richest fire in the world! I'll steal and steal until I steal the whole world. And what will I do with the world once I steal it? I'll burn it! That's what fires do!"

Fire laughed diabolically and burned for twenty-six more days. Finally, only embers lay around him, and he consulted with the one near a stone. "Wait a minute," he stuttered, "I'm part of the world. If I burn up it up, I'll destroy myself! Maybe burning up the world isn't such a good idea. I like to have fun, but I don't want to die having it!"

Fire sat down on a hot stump to think it over.

Meanwhile, Great Lake heard that Fire wanted to steal money. She realized that, with funds, he could burn down the world. "That hothead!" she sputtered. "I'm part of the world, too. I don't want to be destroyed. I don't want to die. Sometimes Fire gets carried away with himself, he doesn't know what to do with all that extra energy. I'll stop him before it's too late."

Beneath her surface, Lake started making waves. "I'll dump my water on his hot stupid head! I'll dampen him real good! He won't destroy me!"

Lake splashed fifty million buckets of water on Fire. A great SSSS sounded through the universe. Soon, Fire's desire to steal millions of dollars fizzled to a thousand, a hundred, twenty, ten, one, and finally to none. Fire's flames relaxed.

"Thanks, Great Lake," he said. "I'm feeling much better. I don't know what came over me. I just got too hot."

Fire smiled at Great Lake. Then he took her by the hand, and they went out for a pizza.

Infant Vision

I T'S SEVEN O'CLOCK, DEAR," Tommy's mother called from the kitchen. The bus will be here in twenty minutes. Put on your shoes."

"Ma, what grade am I in this year?"

"First grade."

"How old am I?"

"Six on your birthday tomorrow."

"Then why do I *look* like eighty-four?"

"You didn't brush your teeth."

"Ma, could I really be eighty-four?"

"You're only six. Be quiet and brush your teeth. You'll be late."

"But Ma—"

"All right, all right. You might be eighty-four tomorrow."

"You mean I can be six *and* eighty-four?"

"Of course. Most people have two ages, some many

more."

"Why?"

"They suffer from infant vision."

". . . What's that?"

"It's the way infants see things."

"Is it good?"

"Sometimes."

"When?"

"When it's pure, fresh, and simple."

"Is that why I'm six but look eighty-four?"

"I don't know."

"Does infant vision run in the family?"

"Your father has it. That's why he jumped out the window when he tried to fly."

"Did he hurt himself?"

"Not exactly. He jumped from the first floor and that was okay. But when he jumped, he forgot to open the window. There's lots of broken glass. He's cut pretty badly—but Dad enjoys hospitals."

"Is that why I'm eight-four today?"

The bus pulled to the curb.

"Put your shoes on," his mother said. "Hurry. Where's your homework assignment?"

"But—how old am I?"

"We'll talk about it after school."

Start Today

I FEEL LOST, ALONE, INADEQUATE, AND INFERIOR," Leslie complained. "Today is my first day as an artist."

"Glum places are pregnant with growth," her husband, Roger, observed.

"But suppose no one ever sees my paintings?"

Roger moved his wife's easel in front of the window. "If that happened, would you still paint?"

"I don't know—"

Leslie lowered herself into the red meditation armchair to ponder. Then she washed some dinner dishes.

Time passed. A month later a spark of optimism flickered in her eyes.

"The idea that no clients will ever see my paintings is actually quite freeing," she said. "Without the outside pressure of an upcoming exhibition, I could rediscover my style, my meaning, my purpose." Excitement rose in her soul. "Time to try again."

"Fading of the old," Roger summarized.

"Yes. And beginning of the new."

"When will you start your new path?"

"Today!"

My Muse

WAITED FOR MY MUSE TO SHOW UP. I like her. When she shows up. She always runs around naked. But it's not as great as it sounds, since I rarely get to touch or catch her.

She's light-footed, lighthearted, and full of fun. But also devilish, mysterious, wildly imaginative. And what about her enigmatic smile?

Finally, she appeared. "Muse, you beauty!" I exclaimed. "I hope you stay with me *forever*."

"I'll do as I please," she warned.

Suddenly, I had a thought: Chains! That's it! I'll chain her to the computer. Then she'll never escape.

I took the chain out of my desk drawer. When her back was turned, I grabbed her, threw her against my keyboard, and chained her up. Ah, at last. Now, beautifully bound to the letter "A," she was mine!

I gazed upon her. Longing and desire flooded my mind. I waited for her to give me an idea . . . but nothing happened.

She laughed. "You idiot! Chains can't hold me. You're wasting your time. Let me go. Keep trying this, and you'll *never* catch me!" She was right. A chained muse means nothing.

Sadly, I released her. Then I asked, "Is there anything I can do to keep you?"

She smiled seductively. "One thing."

"Yes?"

"Forget me."

"How can I do that? I *need* you."

That enigmatic smile again. "Forget me," she repeated, and strolled out the door.

For a week I felt depressed. I shopped for clothing and food, read parts of a novel, jogged, watched TV, and took many walks.

A month passed.

One morning, I awoke feeling fresh, and went straight to my desk.

Voilá! She was standing next to my chair, naked and beautiful as ever. "I never expected to see you again!" I said. She was so alluring. How could I have forgotten her?

She pointed to the blank screen on my monitor. "Sit down," she commanded. "Get to work."

"Yes, ma'am!" I said. And I wrote this piece.

Wow, Look at That!

ONCE UPON A TIME THERE WAS A LITTLE GIRL, full of awe and wonder, who always said, "Wow, look at that!" When she looked at the sidewalk, she'd point down and shout, "Wow, look at that!" When she saw a car pass by or an airplane overhead, she'd point to it and cry, "Wow, look at that!" When she spotted a bird, mouse, dog or cat, flower or tree, pony, man, woman or child, she'd gaze at them with eyes aglow and exclaim, "Wow, look at that!"

One day, a bad fairy flew through the window of the little girl's house and told her, "You're a stupid moron! What is wrong with your brain? Don't you know it's impolite to shout, 'Wow, look at that!'? Worse, it is *wrong*. The things you are pointing at are ugly and bad. You're a silly fool to think otherwise. Be *suspicious* of what you see. Things are not the way they seem. Dogs get old, cats die, chickens get roasted, flowers fade, children age, old men and women abandon you, cars break down, planes get rusty, mice get run over and rot on the street. The world is full of misery. Remember that next time you want to say, 'Wow, look at that!'"

The girl felt terrible. How could she have been so stupid and wrong? She began looking at the world differently. She soon said nothing when she left the house. Her daily smile quickly faded. Her eyes grew dead. And the expression on her face soon resembled a pancake after it has been squashed by a bus.

She got sadder and sadder. But she couldn't even cry, because she now thought that smart, sophisticated little girls didn't do that sort of thing.

One day she finally hit bottom. She lay down on her living room floor, fell asleep, and had a dream about the sun. It reminded her that, once upon a time, her world had been filled with awe and wonder. What had happened?

Then another fairy appeared. "Hello," it said. "I'm the good fairy. The bad fairy and I work together. We teach little girls about life. We're really the *same* fairy, but we wear disguises and try to fool you by looking different. The bad fairy teaches you to feel bad and sad until you reach the bottom of her dark, dreary, nightmare cellar. But there in the darkness, you'll find a strange twisted root. It contains a secret nutrient that, when you eat it, gives you confidence. When you wake up after that, you know for certain that the best way to leave home is with the words: 'Wow, look at that!'"

Paul's Piano Lesson

*C*AN'T WE HURRY THIS BEETHOVEN SONATA?" Mrs. Paythos asked at Paul's piano lesson. "He'll be eleven years old soon, and he's a goal-oriented boy."

"Absolutely not!" Mrs. Wegricht straightened in her seat. "Slowly is the way to go."

"What?" Paul cried, jumping up from the piano. "You must be mad. I *hate* slow!"

"Play it slowly," Mrs. Wegricht demanded.

"*I will not*! Music must have *goals*. When I play the Beethoven 'Pathetique,' my goal is to *finish* it! That's why my fingers fly so fast. It's a *contest*. First pianist to finish wins. I play to win!"

Mrs. Wegricht blew her nose. "That's pretty silly," she sneered. "Luckily your mother pays me good money to tolerate your boorish attitudes. Otherwise, I'd take your piano and stuff it down your ungrateful throat!"

Mrs. Paythos broke in. "You have no reason to berate

my son. Paul's belief about this has brought me many benefits. Last week, for example, when he took up dancing, he
waltzed to the store to buy our groceries!"

"Goal-oriented attitudes belong in the sewer!" Mrs. Wegricht hissed. "You are crass, crass. I've never heard such
nonsense. Luckily, you pay well. Otherwise my high standards could not be compromised."

"That's easy for you to say, Mrs. Wegricht," said Paul,
looking up from the slice of watermelon he was forcing between the piano keys. "Not everyone can attend the Laptop
Computer School of Music as you did, or graduate summa
cum laude from its fruit department."

"What's your *hurry*?" Mrs. Wegricht asked, her face a
frozen mix of scorn and sympathy. "*Hold* each note. *Smell*
it. Feel and embrace it in your hand's mind. Do this, and
Ludwig will love you."

"I don't care about love, or Beethoven, or any of those
creeps. I'd rather crush a note than love it. I play to win, I
tell you!"

"You mean you want to beat Billy McKenzie?"

"Absolutely. I want to banish his 'Pathetique' from this
Earth, grind his fingers to a pulp with my heel, sink him into
last place!"

"Paul, the judges won't like that attitude. I suppose your
next question will be how play the 'Entrepreneurial Sonata.'"

". . . Did Beethoven write that?"

"No, I believe it was his son," Mrs. Wegricht sneered.
She paused a long moment to think about her business prac-

tices. After deciding to keep her student, she quieted herself and calmly said, "Music isn't about competition. It's about expressing your feelings. That's why you must turn off your mind, dive straight into the heart of each sonata, and rubato your way to the top. There, the crown of glory shines and waits for you at the pinnacle!"

Paul paid no attention. "The hell with feelings!" he shouted as he pushed peanut butter between the keys. "The only musical feelings I like are *forte* and *crescendo*. I play them to kill the opposition, I'll happily hammer a scale on Billy's disgusting corpus, or explode an arpeggio in his face to blow him to smithereens. It's no difference to me what happens to that worm. I'd like to dynamite him out of existence."

"My, you are a *violent* student. Placing yourself in such a prison of warped goals is an insult to music. Using our beautiful notes as a weapon, my boy, will bring you neither happiness nor satisfaction." Mrs. Wegricht sighed, rose from her seat, and began to pace the room. Holding her index finger high to trace her wise observations in the air, she declared, "Although pathless may be a creative choice and direction, formless is not. Beethoven knew this. That's why he chose the sonata form. You should consider the feelings of the composer and follow the dynamics of his choice."

Paul was about to shout again, but something in the tone of the word "sonata" stopped him. He sat still, hands over the keys, pensively drifted inward, and, when his thoughts cleared, bent toward his teacher and whispered, "Mrs. Wegricht, my mother won't stand for this. Neither will my father, who lives next door. They don't like feelings. They're dead set against them. Although they can tolerate rage, even a bit of envy and jealousy, they can't stand laughter and tears, and they hate joy, especially when expressed in public on the piano. They also keep complaining about being broke." He lowered his whisper to *pianissimo*. "My parents are, basically, very boring, stupid, narrow, closed-off people. They like their privacy and only give me piano lessons to get me out of the house."

Mrs. Wegricht was paying close attention. "I can understand that," she said. "It's reasonable and traditional. Beethoven had a similar personality. That's why it's so important to play him well. It will help you understand your parents, and you may even learn to like them."

"You sure know your musicology," Mrs. Paythos murmured from her seat in the corner.

"Yes, I do. That's why I know it is best for your son to dive straight into his 'Pathetique.' He should play it slow and juicy, with free-form feeling and thus ecstasy, and rubato his way to winning next month's competition. If he wins, he'll pocket the five thousand dollars in prize money as well as achieve glory among his peers and elders."

During the next two weeks Paul practiced his 'Pathetique' three hours a day. On the day of the competition, he played the piano three miles an hour faster than Billy McKenzie, breaking the New Jersey piano-playing speed limit for eleven-year-olds. The judge, having been high on speed himself as a youth, was quite impressed. "The kid is the fastest in Bergen County!" he muttered.

But the votes of the four other judges won him first prize. They marveled at Paul's ability to play with such passion and self-expression. One of them swooned, "I've never heard such mature playing from a young person!"

Paul passed hundreds of cheering fans as he walked to the stage to receive his award. He shook the chief judge's hand and bowed to the audience. When he descended from the platform, he saw his mother and father sitting next to Mrs. Wegricht, and raced over.

He hugged his parents before handing them his award money.

Then he gave Mrs. Wegricht a big kiss.

Tom and the Hebrew Letters

TOM, A SEVEN-HUNDRED-FOOT-TALL GIANT born with feathers on his legs, couldn't fly because he suffered from stupidity.

Ashamed of his condition, he looked for a teacher to guide him up the Smart and Self-Improvement Ladder. Deep in his undeveloped brain, he knew he could use his massive body as a springboard to a higher state. The only question was how.

On Monday morning, he visited Mrs. Dolan's Landslide Academy of Torah, Talmud, Calligraphy, and Hebrew Letters. The smartly dressed, gray-haired teacher took him by the hand, smoothed his ruffled leg feathers, and taught him how to draw the Hebrew letter aleph on the schoolyard using a hundred-foot Bentworth shovel-tipped pen. Tom towered above the Academy as he drew the first diagonal line of aleph, then added hooked curves on its upper right and lower left.

Suddenly, his aleph burst into flame! Smoke and fire shot out in all directions. The entire letter rocketed into the sky, zoomed in concentric circles around a cloud before turning back and, in a paralyzing line descent, headed straight for Tom's head! In a flash of blinding light, it entered his left ear, burned the center of his brain, inflamed his cerebellum, cerebrum, and medulla, and lit his eyes with a fiery passion.

"Good for you, Tom!" Mrs. Dolan chortled. "Now you understand the nature of aleph!" She loaded three cookies onto a derrick and hoisted them up to his eager mouth. "These sweets are your temporary reward, a small pleasure. But no pleasure can compare to the joy of learning a Hebrew letter! Next we'll try *beth*."

Tom painted *beth* on the schoolyard pavement. When he finished, *beth* burst into flame and rocketed into the sky. Tom gaped in amazement as *beth* somersaulted over a United Airlines air path. Suddenly, it turned around and, in a paralyzing line descent, headed straight for Tom's head! *Splat*! *Beth* landed in his mouth! It burned his tongue, singed his esophagus, charred his throat, and peppered his stomach with burning ash before heading back to his brain, where it vibrated next to the aleph. His eyes shone with *beth's* light of white letter-learning passion.

Next came gimel. Tom painted it in the schoolyard with his Bentworth shovel-tipped pen. But gimel didn't catch fire. It froze in place, hardened into iron, and sank through the concrete. He watched it disappear under the schoolyard.

And then he heard the rumble of an earthquake! The

schoolyard burst open, and gimel, covered with molten lava, shot skyward. It rocketed through the sky, searching for a landing place. It spied Tom. Like a falling star, gimel shot straight down and zinged through his right eye, filling his brain with molten lava, electricity, and magnetism before nestling next to aleph and *beth*.

Every day, Tom painted another Hebrew letter. After twenty-two days, he had mastered the entire alphabet. At night, fire from the Hebrew letters in his eyes lit up the town. Like a lighthouse, it shone for miles around.

Mrs. Dolan was pleased with her student's progress. So was Tom, who had gone from dumb to smart in twenty-two days. On the twenty-third day, the feathers on his legs moved to his arms. He flapped them like wings, and his giant body began to soar. Ascending skyward, he flew through space, toward a higher cloud of Hebrew sentences.

How Tom Typed His Way
to Cold Turkey

THE WINNER OF THE TYPING CONTEST would get a free trip to Turkey. Tom entered. He'd always wanted to see the poppy fields.

When the gun went off, forty contestants began typing. "Thumbs" Goldberg flew at incredible speed; "Thirty Fingers" Halligan soon pulled into the lead at three hundred words a minute. Content was superfluous; only speed counted.

Tom won by pulling out Halligan's electric typewriter plug, turning over Goldberg's table, and pouring glue on the keys of the comma virtuoso Luke Looseness.

"Congratulations, Tom," said Mr. Keys, who'd organized the contest. Using pantomime techniques perfected at the University of Serif, he handed Tom a paw of imaginary stubs. "Here are two tickets to Turkey via Typing Carriage.

Just put your clothes in the roller, and you'll be off."

"What?" said Tom, pushing aside the proffered hand. "I want the real thing! Give me a real trip, or I'll turn you in for pushing dope."

Mr. Keys drew back. "Call in the Lettermen!" he cried. Four Letters entered the room. "Take this young man and put him on the first plane to Turkey. He wants the real thing."

"North Turkey?" asked the short Letterman, dressed like a zero.

"Exactly," answered Mr. Keys.

What a surprise it was for Tom when his plane landed in the Pontic Mountains of Northern Turkey. Snow was falling, and a chilling north wind shook the needles on the pine trees. "I'd better slow down," he said through chattering teeth.

Tom stayed a month. During that time, he kicked his fast-typing habit cold turkey.

Tom's Job

Tom's JOB WAS TO CREATE THE WORLD. He rolled in bed, causing earthquakes in his mattress springs and a few primordial oceanic waves.

But it was too early, and nothing worked.

He turned to his favorite madame, Mrs. Coffee, and drank up her delicious elixir. Bubbles bounced in his stomach, endorphins poured into his spiritual eye-tunnel. Soon he was ready to bereshit.

Meditating on his archetypical caffeine, whose water had originated during the great biblical flood, he thought about Noah, his ancestor, who had practiced putting couples in health-giving, loving, and long-lasting relationships.

Tom began every morning this way.

His job was to create the world.

Middle Road

TOM BROUGHT HIS BLUE BALLOON to the park. He tossed it into the wind and watched it float upwards. Suddenly, his right index finger floated away, too!

Tom was not used to his body parts floating into space without him. He liked control. His eight-year-old body and mind seized the moment: That floating index had to stop!

But how does one control a rebel finger?

He watched helplessly as his index traveled an independent route, separating from the balloon and rising even higher. Passing a cumulus cloud, it crossed San Diego Bay, passed over Nevada, and headed over the Rockies before reversing itself and returning to San Diego.

Then it pointed straight at him. He saw the digit vibrating clearly, its skin glistening and wet from its passage through the cloud.

Then the finger spoke. "Oh, mortal Tom, traveling lost and alone through this confusing world. You may fool others, but you can't fool me. You can't run from me, either. Your hiding days are over. I'll find you wherever you are. That's why it is best to travel the Brutally Honest Road running past jagged cliffs, immense boulders, cactus thorns, poisonous snakes, savage lions, and caterpillars bursting with the iron of butterflies. But fear me not. Fear creates more fear, but the Brutally Honest Road, radiant with awareness, eats up fear and turns it into a friend."

"That's very interesting," said Tom, "but Mr. Fear smells awfully weird. I don't like him."

"Not many do. Nevertheless, when you meet him along the way, say hello, talk to him, and invite him into your mind kitchen for milk, cookies, and ice cream. You'll soon get to know each other. You may even become best friends. You'll see that the Brutally Honest Road is nothing to hide from; it's not as brutal as you thought. More brutal is the Hiding Road, where darkness, fog, and confusion lead to the Land of the Lowly, located just south of Camden, New Jersey."

Tom's index finger floated down to Earth and whispered into his ear, "Don't worry, I'll point things out. I'll be in your hand again once you know the way."

Tom contemplated the space by his ring finger, where the index once sat. He pulled down his balloon, deflated it, and put it in his pocket. He stared at a house across the street, some bushes, then a maple tree. Where should he turn? He began to walk around the park, looking for the future in the palm of his hand.

An hour later, when he returned to his spot, he saw his index finger pointing towards Middle Road.

Tom Graduates
From Criticism School

TOM FINALLY GRADUATED from Criticism School. It took
many years.

Here's the story: As a first grader in the School of Elementary Criticism, arrows of criticism pierced his body, affecting his manner of walking, talking, thinking, and feeling.

A few years later, during his attendance at the High
School of Secondary Criticism, he developed protective
armor. Nevertheless, although most arrows were now deflected, the sound of their ping and ring as their iron tips
glanced off his protective Mogen David shield still affected
the way of life.

This continued through graduation from the College of
Higher Criticism, where he received a Ph.D. in Protoplasmic
Pin-Cushion Maintenance from Dr. Dolor in the Bilious Department. This degree meant he had mastered the art of

inner confidence.

Two weeks after graduation, though he still saw arrows of criticism whizzing by, he was able to toss away his shield. True, he felt their breeze, but otherwise he hardly noticed them. Bilious barbs, once so sharp and frightening, had turned into puffy clouds.

With clear sky above him, he strolled with swinging arms, feet rolling, and brain released, into the smiling freedom of the wide-open countryside.

Tom and the Bogomiles

TOM WONDERED ABOUT his twelfth-century links to the Bogomiles. Did these medieval mystics really dance so well? Could their meditative practices and spiritual discipline, developed in their mountain monastery, really create such mighty powers, enabling high *kopanica horo* leaps, *ruchenitsa* jumps, and Petro Podkovich's *paidoushko* hops? And what about Bogdan Marcovich's exotic *pravo* squats, danced in midnight ecstasy outside Rila monastery walls?

What was their secret?

Was it just a folktale? Or could Bulgarian monks really hop that high?

Tom's mother wondered about his sanity. Could the lad be a Balkan soteriological genius? Or did he actually descend from an ancient Mysian ape family with loose brain cells?

"Ma, I *like* elevation. That's why I love to hop."

"That's nice."

"Remember last month when we danced in the streets of Koprivshtitsa? My party was so much fun! I'm so glad I was born. Thank you." Tom kissed his mother. "Can I hop up the stairs now?"

"*Hoping* is the correct word," she said. "Not hopping. Although both words concern elevation, children often get them confused. Hopping raises the body, but hoping elevates the soul."

"That's nice to know."

"Tom, not every child gets the opportunity to hop in Koprivshtitsa, and dancing there is top of the line. Even Grandpa likes to hop, leap, and jump."

"Well, I like hopping."

"Hoping is the word."

"I'd rather hop than hope. My hopes sank after Grandma heard me play guitar yesterday. She said I stank. I stomped on her toe, but she insisted she was right. Then she twisted my ear. 'Go home and practice!' My ears are still ringing. She screamed it straight into my semi-circular canal!"

"Stomping Grandma isn't nice."

"I hate her. She smashed my hopes. I spit on her shoes, too. I'm never going to practice again!"

"Spite and spit will only hurt you. Grandma wants you to improve."

Tom sighed. "I'm sinking into the swamp. I'm getting nowhere in this world. We played baseball after my birthday party, and I missed the ball seven times. Only the mosquitoes liked it. Maybe ten years old is my final age."

His mother shot him an iron glance. "Stop feeling sorry for yourself! Get back to practicing. Hope and improvement go together. These disciplines feed each other."

"Well, I'm pretty hungry."

"Listen to your Grandma: Discipline, coupled with stringent effort, will lift you out of the swamp."

"She never said that."

"Well, she meant it. In any case, spite energy is a waste of power. And save your spit for digestion. Besides, using either on Grandma, yourself, or anyone else is just a distraction."

"But I love to spit and spite."

"Your father and I don't want you to waste your birthday. Ten years old means time to change. The first double digit is a

magic number with hidden meanings. It's time to use your obstructions and obstacles as stepping stones. Up the ladder to Good-in-Itself Land you go. Start climbing. You'll not only satisfy yourself but bring happiness to the world."

"Good-in-Itself? Didn't Immanuel Kant say that?"

"Smart lad. He also said results are up to the Lord."

"Grandma said that, too."

"Of course. She reads Kant."

"Really?"

"Yes. And she also plays flute. She knows a lot."

"I still feel discouraged."

"Well, feel it, and feel it deeply. It can even become a strange kind of friend, if you get to know it well. After all, courage, dis-courage, giving up—they're all part of the game. But they are never a reason to stop practicing. So often these obstacles are illusions, and like clouds of passing gloom, they soon drift away. Once the sky clears and the sun comes out, it's like nothing happened."

"What about storms?"

"If it rains, buy an umbrella."

"Suppose I slip."

"Lubricate your fingers with scales and arpeggios. That's

worthwhile slipping. Follow your music command-ments. Get better one spark at a time. Let your strings vi-brate with Carcassi, Carulli, Bach, Tarrega, and Sor. Your happy songs will shine on everyone around you."

"You think so?"

"Absolutely. Your best reality is practice, practice. It makes you your own hero."

"You're a wise mama."

"That's because I practice."

"I didn't know you played an instrument."

"I play you."

"Really?"

His mother smiled.

King Diamond

ADAM HAUSNER SOLD DIAMONDS on Forty-eighth Street, in his narrow store squeezed between a diamond emporium and a Greek restaurant. Merchants, hundreds of potential customers, cyclists, pedestrians, police, motorists, tourists, prostitutes, shoppers, and assorted kings and queens from all walks of life paraded daily up and down the street.

Adam was something of a philosopher. Often he drove to work early—before the rush of the city descended on his narrow preserve—and sat behind his small desk in the back of his store. From this position, away from the display cases of diamonds, necklaces, rings, and the green carpeting, and with the tranquility that only a good night's sleep can bring, he liked to take a step backward onto Philosophy Street in the city of his mind. There he wandered aimlessly, wondering about the nature of the world. Was life really a waking dream? Who had created customers? Who had created diamonds? Who had created Adam?

He never came up with answers. Often, just as he was getting close to understanding the relationship between body, mind, and spirit, he would be interrupted. One day it was by a heavy-set man with dark glasses in a black over-coat, who came through the door, pointed at the display case, and asked, "Whaddaya gettin' for dis stone?"

Adam looked at the diamond, set in a gold ring. "Eighteen hundred dollars."

The customer glared at Adam, grunted, turned, and walked out without a further word.

Adam returned to his thoughts. What was the real nature of a diamond? he asked himself. Then it struck him! The diamonds he sold had no intrinsic value. They were, rather, reflections of inner worth, symbols of the "real diamonds" people searched for in themselves.

He was selling reflections.

So, in a sense, his business was superfluous. Was he a fraud? Maybe he should have listened to his father and become a teacher. Then he could have given people something useful, guided them, helped them find their lost parts. His father knew value; he could tell the difference between a lasting truth and a bauble with an ephemeral shine.

Another thought came to him: People owned "real diamonds," but they weren't aware of them. And the few who were didn't know how to find them. By selling his precious stones, Adam was performing a social service for his customers. He was supplying them with reminders.

His brain was really cooking that morning. He thought

up new copy for his next ad: "When you're feeling down and out, remember your diamond within."

He unlocked the display case, picked out his most valuable DeBeers gem, and slipped it into his vest pocket, just above his heart.

He drove home in a good mood that evening. When he hit a traffic jam on the Long Island Expressway, he turned on the radio and listened to Bach while exhaust fumes and waiting cars piled up around him.

After a fifteen-minute wait, the traffic began to move again. He cruised through Queens. At the Great Neck sign, he patted his vest pocket. There was nothing there.

He began to tremble. Where was it? Hadn't he put it in his vest pocket? Or had he? He couldn't remember.

With sweating hands, he searched his pockets but found nothing. His mind flew back to the store. Mentally, he combed the display cases, desk drawers, safe, the rows of catalogs lying open on his desk. It was all a blank.

He pulled over to the side of the road and stopped to search the front seat, the glove compartment, the floor. Still nothing. He panicked. Where could it be? How could he have misplaced—or, worse, lost—such a valuable jewel?

He finished the drive a physical wreck and slumped in his living room armchair, unable to touch the martini his wife brought him.

He gazed into space. Try to remember . . . try to remember. His finger inadvertently slid over his breast pocket. Try . . . there it is! He touched it. His diamond had been with him all along, safe and secure. How could he have forgotten where it was?

He held his hand over his heart. He pressed gently against the precious stone and resolved never to forget it again. Then he fell fast asleep.

"Dinner's ready!" Laura had prepared a huge spaghetti repast. All three kids charged down the stairs, jumped into their chairs, and began grabbing food. "Wait a minute!" Laura snapped. "Don't be pigs! Wait until everyone is seated."

Adam yawned, stretched, and took slow, leisurely strides toward the dinner table. The kids eyed him eagerly. As soon as he sat down, they dove for the food. "Where are your manners?" Laura shouted. The kids started yelling at each other.

Adam's peace of mind vanished. "Shut up around here!" he said, slamming his fist on the table. "I want quiet when I eat!"

"Listen to your father," Laura whispered.

The dinner continued in silence until Liam, the eldest son, dumped his plate of spaghetti on the floor and ran upstairs.

Adam's appetite disappeared along with the spaghetti, which he forced Liam to clean up and flush down the toilet.

He took a walk around the block to help digest what little food he had eaten. As he passed the candy store, the old panic returned. *Where was his diamond?* He wanted to touch it, see it, feel it. He wanted to remember how valuable he was. But he kept forgetting. And when he did, a terrible panic ensued, a heavy cloud darkening his world. He felt like a fool, weak, even stupid. Why must a grown man need to touch a diamond for hope, security, sustenance, self-knowledge, and wisdom? Did everyone need a diamond as he did?

He bought four halvah bars in the candy store and raced down the dark side street, tearing off wrappers and shoving the bars into his mouth one after another. He hardly chewed them.

The sudden rush of sugar softened his fear and gave him hope. But the energy surge soon ended on a low plane of lethargy and despair. He had lost it again. He sat on a park bench. The night air was cool and clear. A breeze blew, then stopped. No cars passed. The leaves above his head were still. Adam listened. His heart stopped pounding. He sighed and slouched forward as his shoulders relaxed. Then he felt the stone moving against his heart. His eyes lit up. Found. Why had he ever been afraid? Why the panic? It had always been there.

Why was it so hard to remember? No matter how many times he tried, he kept forgetting. His treasure lay, always and forever, deep within him. But he needed diamonds to remind him.

He headed home along the darkened streets, thinking about reminders.

Paying Off a Loan

CHARGED INTO THE BANK MONDAY MORNING, frantically looking for money to pay off the loan shark swimming behind me. The teller said, "Go downstairs to the vault." I took the stairs three and four at a time with the shark snapping at my heels.

Luckily the vault was open. I raced in, tripped over a bag of coins, and fell headlong into a pile of cash. With a feeling of relief, I gathered the piles together and stuffed them in the loan shark's mouth. His huge jaws snapped greedily at the greenbacks. When he'd had enough, he swam clumsily out of the vault and up the stairs. His fin got stuck in the revolving door, but he escaped down Ocean Avenue.

I sat in the remaining pile of cash, sweating. That was a close call, I thought.

Just then, a beautiful woman came toward me. She had long blond hair down to her waist and a lithe, slender figure. Her skirt was very tight and had cash receipts printed all over it. Her legs were so close together, I could easily tell she was the bank mermaid.

"What are you doing here?" she gasped. "Help! Help! A robber!"

"Please! Please don't shout," I said. "My ears are very sensitive to pressure. I'm not a bank robber. I only came in for a quick loan. I had to pay off a debt in a hurry, and now that I have, I feel much more relaxed. Perhaps you'll sit down and we can talk?"

She looked me over hesitantly, then calmed down as she realized I was harmless. "We've had a lot of robberies lately," she said, perching on a stack of hundred-dollar bills. "I guess I'm a bit jittery."

We sat discussing the banking business, foreign currency, and the falling value of the dollar for half an hour. "Imagine," I laughed. "Soon those hundreds you're sitting on will be just about worthless."

"Yes," she answered. "It's a real problem. Sitting on dollars won't keep inflation down."

Her name was Esther. I wrote down her phone number as we left the bank together. We saw each other over the next few days. I was so happy to be free from debt. Now I could love again. And what a beautiful woman I had to love! It made me realize that banks can offer more than just money. On Friday afternoon, when I went to the bank to meet her, I suddenly saw the loan shark coming after me again. "What do *you* want?" I growled. "I just paid you off!"

"Like hell you did!" said the shark angrily. "Those dollars you gave me ain't worth nothin' no more. I wanna be paid off in gold. Ain't you heard about inflation?"

The old panic instantly returned, and I started to run with the shark snapping at my heels. How could I repay him? I ran toward the bank—it was my only hope! I charged through the revolving door and dashed down the stairs, leaping three and four at a time. Luckily the vault was still open. I raced in, tripped over a bag of gold coins, and fell headlong into a pile of cash. "Take the coins," I yelled. "Take the coins!"

I picked up handfuls and shoved them into his greedy mouth. I could hear his sharp teeth grinding them into dust. As he swallowed, I knew that, soon, his digestive enzymes would compact that dust into gold bars.

Finally, the shark had had enough. He swam clumsily out of the bank and down Ocean Avenue. I remained in my pile of cash, waiting for Esther.

When she arrived, she looked concerned. "What happened?" she asked. "I was worried about you."

"The shark was after his money again," I said. "But don't worry. I gave him the gold in the vault. He's satisfied now." I wiped my sweating brow with my handkerchief. "Why don't we go out to supper together?"

"Good idea." She took my hand. "You've had a rough day."

I agreed. We headed for a nearby seafood restaurant, entered the back room, and sat down in a quiet corner.

"Relax," said Esther in a soothing voice. The waiter was soon bringing out orders. "It's all over now. Put your mind at ease, and eat your fish." She looked closely at my plate. "Hmm," she hmmed thoughtfully. "Looks like shark."

I studied my plate for a long moment. "You're right," I said, gleefully jabbing my fork into it. That night I ate with a vengeful smile of satisfaction.

Florence

FLORENCE TURNED HER HEAD toward Fred. Her blue eyes burned into his sockets. "Fred," she said, "you know my struggle. After I read *Paradise Lost*, I decided to battle God for control of the Earth. Today I am still fighting. It's tough. God is everywhere, and I am nowhere. This fight may take my whole life."

Fred shrugged. "Who am I to question God?" he asked. "Why don't you go back to Jamie's Meat Market? Being a butcher made you happy. It gave you a feeling of fulfillment. What happened? Did it become just another job?"

"I still *like* butchering. But I wanted to go beyond cows, sheep, pigs, and chickens. I wanted to expand big time. That's why I took such a low-paying job with Satan, Inc. They swear they'll put God out of business in five years. They've got fourteen branches in the city already and expect to open in the suburbs next year."

"Fine job for a young woman," Fred mused.

She agreed. "I want to be president someday."

He looked concerned. "I hope you'll be happy. Such high expectations can lead to lots of frustration."

"I don't expect to fail," she assured him.

Nonsense Path

WHERE DOES THE NONSENSE PATH LEAD? No one knows. But it calls me. Doors can open through the unexpurgated writing of nonsense. But walking the irrational Nonsense Path cannot be a goal. Goals destroy the path by making sense. Nonsense travels concealed in darkness; it is often the way of disaster, dynamite, and the devil.

But the path leads to Luminescent Land, where nonsense brightens the day! A walk on it can't be planned. Best is to unleash the mind. Let it wander the fields and hills, unearth secret turnips, ostrich eggs, phosphorescent worms, and rocks pitted with gold.

The Nonsense Path often reveals hidden plans behind the world's apparitions.

The Wind and the King

ONCE THE WIND VISITED A CASTLE. The King walked out to meet her and fell in love. "Let's get married," he said.

The Wind answered, "Join me first. Let's play in the wild universe together."

"Ah, I would love that," said the King. "But I live in a castle. What will happen to my subjects? They can't live without a king. I can't live without them. Instead, let's build a new castle for you *and* my kingdom."

The Wind thought about her loss of freedom and the responsibilities of a ruler. A great guy, she concluded, but not for me.

Having learned his lesson, he never fell for the Wind again, and he outlawed all breezes in a fit of pique.

Hystation: He Wasn't There

IS HYSTATION A PREVENTABLE DISEASE or a natural part of the life cycle? This question was proposed by Dr. Kinnewhat at the opening meeting of the Society of Invertebrates in the Salt Marsh Estuary, Massachusetts. Several frogs in the audience croaked when he proposed his theory of cyclic indifference, but the cheering tadpoles drowned them out.

A generational split over the issue was taking place.

As the commotion subsided, the doctor pulled up his shirt, revealing a large gurp on his chest. "This is what happens when you're at the bottom of your cycle," he said, fondling the gurp. "The energy just drains out of you. You feel like a shell of your former self."

As he spoke, you could see his body beginning to unravel. His energy was draining fast. His inverted brain began pouring its contents down his spinal cord and collecting in fetid hystation pools. It looked as if someone was pulling the threads of his skin apart. His legs grew shorter, his torso shriveled, his arms fell off, and his face collapsed.

As the symposium beheld the hystation taking place, one of the frogs tried saving the doctor's brain. He hopped to the lectern and reached for it with his tongue but was too late. Only the thought of the doctor remained.

"Where *is* he?" shrieked the frog's wife.

An after-image flashed behind the lectern, and a frog shouted, "There he is!" The audience turned to look . . . but he wasn't there.

Mama Clock

MAMA CLOCK LED HER SON, Ben, down the road. She had his wrists tied to a watch and his brain strapped to a schedule. Although Ben lived in a lovely village surrounded by trees, fresh air, and flowers, he couldn't see its beauty. Too tied down, he dwelt in Time Prison, handcuffed and ruled by Mama.

She controlled him. There was no deviation from her schedule. Every day was exactly the same; changes came only once a month, on Sundays. If Ben avoided his schedule, Mama Clock would shake her rusty fist, twist her tin face into a scowl, and shout, "Moron, get back on schedule! I'm not ticking away here to amuse you. You can only pull yourself out of your swamp by following my schedule. It will tell you exactly what to do, and your wristwatch will tell you exactly when to do it. Follow my advice. Until you can run your own life, I will run it for you!"

Mama Clock called Ben stupid so often that he eventually believed it. He became a docile and willing prisoner. The thought of freedom frightened him.

One day he met a thin, lively girl with dancing blue eyes. Her name was Frieda. She had a spirited way of talking, laughed easily, seemed unafraid, and had a good time wherever she went.

"Why can't I have fun, too?" he asked Mama Clock.

"You're too dumb for fun."

But Frieda thought Ben was just as smart as anybody else. "Mama Clock wants to keep you prisoner by *convincing* you you're stupid," she told him. "If she keeps you handcuffed to your wristwatch, you won't find out how smart you are."

Ben had many talks with Frieda. After lunch, they'd walk in the park or sit by the ocean, watching the waves roll in. As he began to understand he wasn't stupid after all, his belief in himself grew.

So did his fights with Mama Clock. Fearing he might break out of Time Prison, she hurled one accusation after another at him. "Stupid, blithering, blundering idiot! Your brain is softer than an egg yolk. How can a moronic, loathsome creature like you expect to succeed in the world?"

Ben defended himself, fought off each accusation with his newfound belief. The more he fought, the more he emerged from Time Prison. He unlocked his wrists, dropped his wristwatch in the gutter, and tore up his schedule. Soon he was able to say goodbye to Mama Clock.

He held Frieda's hand as they danced down the road together.

Mama Clock screamed when she lost her son. When that didn't work, she shook her fists. When that didn't work, she calmed down. Taking a few easy breaths, she muttered, "Finally," to herself. She smiled.

Then she waved to her son. "Good luck, Ben," she said. "And have a good time!"

Salvation Menu:
Driving the Wild Horse

JACK WAS BORN WITH A WILD HORSE IN HIS HEAD. Neighbors claimed his mother had put it there. Or perhaps it was Uncle John from Bergenfield. Or maybe he'd been born with it. Nobody knew for sure. But no matter who or what had done it, Jack grew up with a wild horse problem.

In the beginning, he blamed his mother. It was easier that way. Every Wednesday, after kindergarten, he'd ask, "Ma, why did you plant this beast in my brain?"

"Your father did it," she would answer

After six years of hearing the same midweek tune, she rebelled. When Jack came home from sixth grade with his usual complaint, she looked him straight in the eye and said, "Jack, stop blaming me. I won't take it anymore. It's not my fault. Horses, foxes, mules, rabbits, whatever—you and you alone are responsible! It's time to take care of your own stable." Softening a bit, she added, "I can understand why you may still want to blame me. After all, I'm taller."

Three days later, after Jack fell out of a window, he began taking more responsibility.

Still, despite weekly consultations with the local therapist, Jack's problem persisted throughout high school and college.

His wild stallion pulled him so much, he often went over the cliff, although sometimes, by holding the reins real tight, he managed to get the horse back on track.

What a mess. What could he do with the beast? How could he control it?

Suddenly, a genie appeared before him and said, "Master, I am here to do your bidding. Whatever you want, you shall have. Tell me your wish, and it shall be granted."

"Wow, pretty good!" Jack exclaimed, reining in his horse. "Who are you? Where did you come from?"

"I'm your reminder," said the genie. "I'm bypassing your distracting questions. Simply know that, though your mind is a wild horse, *you* are its driver."

"Hey, genie, you think I'm some kind of moron?" snarled Jack, feeling the sting of insult. "Who sent you? My mother?"

The genie, smarting equally from insult, raised his hand to strike the lad. "You young ingrate! I'll—"

"Hold your horses!" Jack chuckled at the irony. "Listen, genie, I *know* that! I know myself better than you think. I know my route is Edge-of-Cliff. On one side are open fields, blue sky, and sunlight; on the other a steep chasm, the abyss of darkness. I know it's a bumpy ride, but I'm holding the reins tight!"

The genie scratched his head. "Pretty good, kid. You're smarter than I thought. Okay, my job is done. I'm off to see my next client."

"*What*? Wait! What will keep me on the road?"

"Your horse! Watch him, but keep the reins in hand. Put yourself on the road to Becoming as you stay on the road of Being. That's the paradox and irony: To be in the present as you see into the future. Striving to get better and improve will straighten out your mind and keep your horse from going over the cliff."

"Anything else?"

"Isn't that enough?"

The Underachiever

WE ARE AN ACHIEVEMENT-ORIENTED SOCIETY. Often, in our unending drive to find success, we leave friendship and family behind.

Let us therefore take a stand here and now for underachievement. Let us proclaim the wisdom of doing less!

Underachievers are everywhere.

Why, even achievers often feel they are underachievers. Just to prove they aren't, they fight to achieve even more.

Support your local underachiever and you will be supporting your friends, family, neighbors, mayor, councilmen, merchants—even your local police.

Underachievers have time: time for friends, for their families, for fun and love. Everyone knows that time is all around us. Yet only the underachiever seems to have enough time to enjoy it.

Underachievers, unite! You have nothing to lose but your facades. The slaves of achievement may work all day and burn bright fires, which many can see, but only the underachiever can enjoy the natural light of the sun.

Brain Arthritis

J ACK'S BRAIN WAS GETTING STIFF. When he spoke, words congealed in his mouth and fell out like sticks. He decided to see Dr. Hartmind, who did an immediate brain scan. "Jack," he said, "you are suffering from brain arthritis. It is a curable disease, but the treatment is very painful."

"So is the pain, Doctor. I'll do anything to get rid of it."

"Good." The doctor nodded. "A positive attitude is important in this treatment. Traditionally, we give our patients only aspirin. However, a laboratory in New Jersey has developed a special drug for the treatment of brain arthritis. It is now available in pill form. At your stage, the disease is so advanced, only concentrated doses can help."

The doctor reached into his drawer and pulled out a small bottle. "Take these pills. They'll make change easier and lessen the pain. Take them every day for one year. After that, you won't need them anymore. You'll be able to change all by yourself."

"Thank you so much," said Jack. "I feel better already."

"That's one of the miracles of these pills," the doctor explained. "You feel better even before you take them."

Jack went home. After lunch he took his first pill, a round white one with a sweet fragrance. Then he left his house for his afternoon stroll. Every day for twenty-three years, he had walked the same street and always turned left at Baker Avenue. That day, however, he decided to turn right!

The pills were working.

He walked past dull red-brick houses. Suddenly, he noticed sparkling window panes, polished handrails, and black-shingled roofs. Maple trees stood proud and straight, their sturdy branches vibrating and dynamic, like powerful hands reaching toward the sky.

He glanced at the street. Even the asphalt shone!

Everything looked so different, so new. The fire hydrant seemed to survey the neighborhood like a conquering general.

Then Jack began to feel uneasy. This was enough adventure for one day. He returned home, sat down in his familiar living room armchair, and opened *A History of the Black Sea Trade; Cumulative Effects on Eleventh Century Expansion During the Byzantine Empire*. The book's 543 pages had been translated from German into English; many sentences went on for two pages and more. Jack began reading, even though the author was a marvel of dullness. He read every word, comma, period, page number, and footnote up to page 34. By page 35, he was almost asleep.

Suddenly, a new daring pumped adrenalin into his stomach. He slammed the book shut and threw it across the room. It smacked against the wall and fell into the waste basket where it belonged. Jack smiled triumphantly. He rose, approached his bookshelf, and picked out *Martin Eden*, by Jack London. Licking his lips, he sat down to read.

In time, Jack began changing many attitudes. He learned to formulate a thought, act on it, and, if it didn't work, try a new one. As he changed and became more flexible, he took fewer pills. Eventually, he didn't even need them. Although, like all those afflicted with brain arthritis, he had occasional relapses, he nevertheless struggled to bring a new vision to each day.

Brain arthritis had loosened its grip on him.

And he had a better grip on life.

Blood Flow

"BLOOD FLOW IS CONTROLLED THROUGH METAPHORS," said Dr. Breathdare to Jason Peabody, who was lying under the Thirty-third Street sign. Blood was oozing out of the wound beneath his sixteenth vertebra, forming a puddle on the sidewalk; yet Jason remained calm. He watched his blood flow south towards Thirty-second Street and meditated upon the Danube and how smoothly it flowed by Slovakia, Hungary, Bulgaria, Romania, and through the Dobruzhian Delta into the Black Sea. His own dark stream was now trickling past Macy's, the IRT subway station, and Madison Square Garden.

Dr. Breathdare kneeled next to Jason and said, with quiet assurance, "You've made your point, Jason. People are beginning to stare at you. It's time to stop this attention-getting behavior and get back to your office. Stop this blood flow *now*!"

Jason concentrated on the command. He clamped his

mind on his arteries and slowed his heartbeat. His wound clotted. "Thank you, Jason," said kindly Dr. Breathdare. "You have performed an outstanding public service. Always better to speak up than bleed in public. People will listen to you."

Jason rose. "Thank *you*, Doctor," he said, picking up his briefcase, and he headed toward his travel office in Penn Plaza. "Now I can finish writing that Eastern European guidebook."

Personality-Changing Meat-Grinding Machine

T HOMAS SUFFERED FROM IPD—Intractable Personality Disorder, a disease he inherited from his mother. How could he become more selfless, caring, sensitive, and open? How could he break out of Ego Prison, with its delicious meals and thoughtful staff?

A Personality-Changing, Meat-Grinding Machine, on sale in Pathmark for $29.95, gave him hope. He jumped into his Mitsubishi and drove off to buy it.

He put the machine on his living room table, dialed *Kind, Sensitive, and Caring*, opened the steel door, put his head inside, and threw the switch. Warm currents heated his brain. When he heard *ping!* he was done. The door opened; out came a new Thomas—kind, sensitive, and caring. There was only one drawback: His head had burnt to a crisp.

Nevertheless, during the next few weeks he grew more and more enthusiastic about his new personality. He told his friends. Some jumped into their cars and headed for Pathmark.

Voice

THAT LOUSY ROTTEN VOICE! Who does he think he is? *Left* me. Just like that! You call that gratitude? And after all I've done for him. I gave him the best place in my body—and he leaves.

I'm not the kind of girl to let just anybody in. I've got my standards. I'm very particular. But this Voice was real nice. You know the type—smooth and soft-sell yet strong and macho, super-masculine yet somewhat laid back. And *oh* so attractive! All the other girls in the office wanted him.

At first, I didn't mind sharing. But after a while I wanted him all to myself. I've got so little time. After working all day typing papers, serving coffee, bringing buns into executive meetings where all those dark-suited creeps clean their hands on my public and private parts—oh, they are disgusting! I hate them! But I had to do it. I had to.

After all, what could I say? I had no Voice.

But then I found my Voice. Ah, sweet Voice. He's protecting me, speaking up for me.

Why should I have to share him with the other girls? Let them find their own voice.

Morgan the Gorgon

ORGAN THE GORGON HAD DIFFICULTY making friends. Snakes grew out of his head; they hissed whenever anyone came near him. Morgan was very upset. The number of snakes was increasing each year.

Finally, in desperation, he went to a snake doctor, who understood his problem immediately. "There is a snake coming out of your head for every evil deed you have committed," he said. "The only way to get rid of them is to reverse the effects of the evil deeds. This is a very difficult task."

"I'll do anything to get rid of the snakes," said Morgan.

"Then follow me to the Room of Mistakes." The doctor led Morgan downstairs to a large underground chamber. As soon as they crossed the threshold, the snakes started hissing furiously. "Shut up!" shouted Morgan. But the snakes kept hissing. He had no control over them.

"If you look through this window," said the doctor,

"you will see the Field of Evil Deeds."

"What evil deeds have I done?" asked Morgan.

The doctor laughed. "There are so many, I don't have time to list them all. Judging from your most prominent snakes, though, you have robbed mailboxes, cheated your friends, lied to your parents, stolen from your classmates, and bullied little children. I see countless others, too." The doctor put his hand on Morgan's shoulder. "You must go to the Field of Evil Deeds," he said. "Uproot every plant you find."

"Will it get rid of the snakes?"

"Absolutely."

As Morgan explored the Field of Evil Deeds, he found that it extended much farther than the doctor's basement. It spread over many city blocks. He couldn't see the end of it. Some plants were taller than he was. One looked like a small tree, with iron blades growing out of its trunk and razor blades instead of leaves. There were cactuses, rose bushes, and nettles. It might take weeks, he thought, to uproot one plant alone.

He got down on his hands and knees, and started weeding. The first plant he pulled up cut his thumb. He worked for hours on a huge cactus; his fingers blistered and bled.

After nine hours of weeding, he had uprooted only four plants.

He fell on the ground, exhausted. It seemed hopeless. But when he awoke, he saw that two of his snakes had fallen out. They lay dead on the ground beside him. Encouraged, he spent the next three days weeding furiously.

He worked in the field, ate in the field, slept in the field. When his hands got bloody, he bandaged them and continued weeding.

He weeded for months. Every few days, another dead snake fell off. After a year had passed, the field was completely cleared.

Morgan felt much better. He visited the doctor again. "Look at yourself in the mirror," the doctor said.

Morgan did. The snakes were all gone. He looked wonderful without them. "Fantastic!" he exclaimed. He was ready to face the world again, no longer as Morgan the Gorgon, but as Morgan the Fair.

Leif Ericsson Meets Lord Berserk

L EIF ERICSSON TAKES HIS ADVENTURE across the fjords, over the green mountains padded with growling grass and poison trees reaching out, touching him, torching him with belly-belching fire from the center of the Earth.

But Leif is unafraid. He trudges among foot bandages and gnarled knee trunks bent at the hip, plopping and piercing, foot after foot, on his unknown way to America. Discoveries are never easy, but what choice is there? Morning sandwiches have not yet arrived. Drinking coffee and eating doughnuts in an American restaurant is no mean feat, especially with the eleventh century watching.

These are stories coated with the wax of ancient times. Vikings peruse a dark hall laden with Byzantine silks and images of pristine Druidic hordes from the Celtic East, where Tartar-running is the mode. Don't stretch too much, else the break comes.

Leif has no friends. Who else is as crazy as he? How can he relate to the mere sanity of these dullards and unadventurous louts living around him? To strike out across lonely, dangerous seas for unknown lands fraught with danger and hard beauty—that is the beatific life of a crazy man.

Leif kneels before his master, Lord Berserk. Dressed in bearskins and with traces of shaving cream still nestled in his beard, the nobleman crowns the bare head of his first and only subject. He declares in a deep, fjordian voice, "Oh, Leif, sail on. Let no nascent whale or bloated walrus dent your enthusiasm for the insane. Let no lackey of dripping blues besmirch your belly-busting visions. You will conquer the world, my lad, and your tools will be blindness and foolishness! Let the dried-up hags of village politics vent their empty rages upon you. Let the empty-nested creators of thatched-roof philosophies rail against you. These mean nothing when a man is on a permanent search for spirit gold. And indeed, my Leif, you shall find it, far away beyond the dark field of seas. Therefore, my son, I give you my bear blessing. Go forth and conquer the black waves of fear, beat the wind with your iron fist, and create a new world on the fir tree ashes of the old."

"Thank you, Lord Berserk," says Leif. "I am sinking into a murky dream. The camouflage beyond the treetops makes no sense. I will conquer the road beyond lands, reach for the path beyond stars. Bless me with your bearskin tunic. My journey will be long and endless, and only burning love and fiery attachments will carry me to the edge."

Theseus

THESEUS GRABBED ARIADNE'S THREAD and headed toward the labyrinth. Stars shone red that night, and the walls of distant turrets percolated under the hot, luminescent Cretan sun.

"It's much better underground," he cried. "Labyrinth walls protect me from sunstroke. But no walls can protect me from the paws of the Minotaur. If I can dance the *syrtos*, will his savage mind be soothed? I cannot be sure. I have never met this creature. He may like Egyptian dances or horas from the Getae of not-yet Romania.

"Perhaps, though, he isn't as bad as others make him out to be. Minotaurs have problems of their own. You can't tell what living in a labyrinth all your life will do to you. Perhaps this one needs someone to talk to, a consciousness-raising group, maybe some peaches from Rhodes. I shouldn't prejudge him, even if he does have horns."

Theseus held onto Ariadne's thread as he danced *syrtos*

into the labyrinth.

Four days later, he met the Minotaur at a bend in the tunnel. "I love *hasapicos*!" roared the Minotaur. "And you know something? I want to retire in Constantinople sometime in the next three thousand years."

Theseus and the Minotaur argued about *hasapicos* versus *syrtos* and the importance of dancing the *Miserlou* in Pittsburgh.

After two days of dance competition, Theseus finally shouted, "*Hasapicos* fans do not deserve to live!"

He piled *syrtos* upon *hasapicos*, slew the Minotaur, and threaded his way back to Ariadne.

Diogenes

THE SECOND-CENTURY GREEK PHILOSOPHER Diogenes Egocentric asked his cousin, Aristotle Unicentric, "What is the most difficult thing in the world?"

His cousin answered, "To be your true self."

Then the philosopher asked, "Is there anything more difficult than that?"

"To be your true self in front of others."

Index Finger Points the Way

TOM NOKLE CAME HOME FOR WINTER BREAK from his senior year in college. As a pre-med student planning to specialize in chiro-therapy, the study of the hand, he had lots of anatomy questions. Eating his eggs at the breakfast table, he asked his mother, a teacher of biology in high school, "In your opinion, what is the purpose of an *index* finger? What's it really used for?"

She adjusted her apron. Standing near the stove, she pointed to his eggs. "Index finger points to the self," she explained. "On a deeper, philosophical level, it is the *ego* finger. As a dual-purpose finger, it can point both forward and back, forward to consciousness, back to *self*-consciousness."

"That's pretty good, Mother. I didn't realize you knew so much."

"Silly child. What about my Ph.D. in metaphysics?"

"Yes, I forgot about that."

"With such a faulty memory, it's no wonder you keep

coming home for guidance."

She stirred her oatmeal. "As the higher finger of consciousness," she continued, "it points to knowledge, union with the universe, and oneness. The index finger never changes. It is always the same, the All-in-One finger. It's my guide through daily life and the universe. That's why I point it at you when you when you do something wrong, or right. It points the way. That's why I love it."

She pointed to her oatmeal.

Tom put down his fork. "I never thought it was so dignified. Our professor in anatomy class just called it a digit."

"That's what they're paid to say by the computer companies and math departments," she sneered. She dipped two pieces of bread into the egg batter that had been sitting there, sprinkled them with cinnamon, slid them into the frying pan, and lowered the flame. "But, paradoxically, especially when pointing backwards—you know, retrogression, selfishness, as opposed to large or divine selfishness, which is really selflessness in disguise—it is also the finger of the self-conscious ego."

She sprinkled a bit more cinnamon on the French toast, waited a moment, then flipped them over. "As such, it creates tension, fear of judgment by others, fear of audiences, fear of the public. It pushes you to show off, prove yourself, and as such, to be different—or *appear* to be—from who you really are. This kind of index-finger pointing is a common problem in humans."

She turned off the flame and, spatula in hand, removed the French toast from the frying pan and laid the pieces on two separate dishes.

"That will always be *your* big challenge," she said. "How to rise above the machinations of your index finger, free yourself from *self*-pointing, and move toward the *objects* your index finger points out."

The aroma of fresh French toast scented the kitchen. Tom got up and paced the floor. "But how long will that *take*, Mother? I don't have all day, you know."

She laid their French toast on the breakfast table.

"You'll be going back to college in two weeks," she continued. "That should give you time to figure it out."

She untied her apron, sat down, and tasted her French toast.

Tom took a bite of his. "Ma, this is delicious. What's in it?"

"I have my own ingredients—a bit of barley, rum, potatoes, and some cheese. But I also add a secret ingredient."

"What's that?"

"It's a secret."

He took another bite and his eyes closed in pleasure. "I love it," he said. "So sweet and juicy, full-bodied and wholesome. "I want to make it for my friends at college."

"Good idea."

"How do I do it?"

"I'll give you the recipe. That will help you cook and create a very good French toast. But the secret, the magic formula that creates this fantastic French toast, I cannot and will not give. The secret stays with me."

"Then how will I cook it on campus?"

"You'll figure it out."

"But—"

"No buts. You have most of the recipe. But that extra fantastic something, you'll have to find it on your own. When you do, your French toast will be just as good. Only different. Do lots of research and thinking. You'll figure it out. Your medical and philosophy courses will help, especially your anatomy-of-the-hand course and your study of digits. You'll find your own way of doing things and, as a future doctor, your own way of treating others. You'll figure it out. Then you'll be making the best French toast ever! Your index finger will point the way."

Tom went off to college and started to make French toast for his friends. His first attempts tasted like burnt rubber. His friends suggested gluing them to his tires. The next time, in frustration, they threw the toast into the garbage can. They threw his new attempts in his face the next day. Then they threw eggs at him. "This has no taste, no magic, no nothing," they sneered. They threw his toaster pan into the garbage can. A day later, they threw Tom into the garbage can, too.

But he wouldn't give up. He kept trying, making French toast for teachers, drunks, and lawyers; he even started handing it out to passersby on the street. But nothing seemed to work. Instead of getting better, his efforts got even worse.

He offered a morning helping to one of the sanitation men, who, after tasting it, said that he was thinking of grinding Tom up with the rest of the garbage.

At that point, Tom realized it was time to change his environment. He left Boston College, tried the University of Chicago, which rejected him, and ending up washing dishes in the kitchen at St. Bridget's College in Olaf, Minnesota.

On Sunday, at the community breakfast, the nuns generously asked him to make his French toast their Sunday communal breakfast. During this experiment in compassion, which they named the First Breakfast, they tasted and chewed with sympathy and compassion. The second time, they added extra spoonfuls of syrup, honey, sugar, or molasses. During the third breakfast, after some nuns vomited across the sanctuary carpet, many thought a good Roman-style crucifixion was in order. (College historians later called this meal the Last Breakfast.)

Tom moved from place to place and was employed over the year in many depressing kitchen and restaurant waiting jobs. But he never gave up. Discouraged, down, he returned to college. After graduating from Dumpster University in Dreary, Colorado, with a fine arts degree in sanitation arrangement, he took his first job as a soussouosousous chef in Dreary's downtown Kato Lakko Diner. After the owner, a kindly man named Aristotle Pappatikkidapoulis, gave him a chance to cook, he offered his French toast to morning patrons.

Three months later, after the owner went bankrupt, Tom was hired by a local mobster and fellow Dumpster graduate, Jonny Bones (aka Dr. Posthumous), to make French toast for his enemies. "I've tried other means of enemy removal for years," he told his associates. "This should do it."

After his first success in Dreary, Tom went international.

His introduced his French toast-making method to France, Turkey, Azerbaijan, and Australia. As his skills improved and governments fell, he kept moving on, always working to perfect his French toast art and hoping he would find the magic formula, the secret ingredient that would make them fantastic.

YEARS WENT BY. One day, at the age of sixty-four, while working as a cook in the restaurant of a three-star hotel in Yerevan, Armenia, Tom was preparing the French toast for his breakfast customers in the Star of Armenia back-alley restaurant.

This time, however, for some strange reason, Tom tried something different. Maybe "tried" isn't the exactly the right word. Rather than being conscious, it seemed to happen naturally, almost effortlessly, by itself, as if it had fallen from the sky, but of course only after years and years of work, false tries, and skewed attempts. It's as if all those years of experience, of suffering, of searching for the culinary clue to excellence, the magic wand of French toast supremacy, the secret ingredient that would catapult his French toast into a superior category—suddenly coalesced . . . into his index finger!

Yes! His index finger had become the vehicle through which the totality of his inner being suddenly expressed itself. When he accidently stirred the French toast batter with his index finger, the power of his whole body poured through it, straight into the batter, imbuing it with the essence of his personality, artistry, creative abilities, his essence and unique view and approach to the world. As this uniqueness entered the batter, he batted it, stirred it around, and thus filled it with the bat-flying creativity of his mind.

And Tom realized that, instead of stirring the batter slowly and carefully with a spoon, what he required was light, fast strokes with his index finger.

Light, even very light, stirring was the key to moving the mental enzymes of fast-jumping "exhilarants" into the batter. This way, when the French toast was cooked, people would immediately be elevated into exhilaration. When his customers took a bite, exhilaration immediately struck. They started dancing! Right after breakfast!

A FEW DAYS LATER, as he was cooking breakfast in the Star of Armenia kitchen, he heard a gigantic roar coming from the dining room. Tom, and the hotel manager, ran out to see what had happened. A man lay on the floor, screaming, laughing, and kicking his legs in the air with joy, a look of utter ecstasy on his face. "Barev, vareev!" he cried "Schnoor-hagalutzion! Schnoorhagalutzion!"

"What's he saying?" Tom asked the manager.

The astonished manager said, "Good, good. Thank you, thank you." The manager broke into a broad smile, laughed joyously, grabbed Tom, shook his hand, hugged him, and started dancing an Armenian hora around the room.

Tom started to cry.

FROM THEN ON, THE ASCENT BEGAN. One success followed another. Restaurants started to clamor for his services.

What was the secret? Why were his toasts so great? *The*

mix. The *mixing* of the ingredients. For years he had mixed the ingredients with his hands. Then he had tried using his fingers, first all of them, then one at a time. The week before, he had tried only that index finger. His whole personality now seemed to point straight through it, and its fluidity and creativity entered directly into the French Toast. *That* was the secret ingredient! His French toast began to flower and sing, shining on the pinnacle of cuisine. And those customers who tasted it tasted not only Tom's years of suffering on the cross of creativity, but the joy of final salvation, where all the worlds of past and present came together in one grand unity.

Armenian, English, Turkish, Bulgarian, even the dead came back to life for a taste of his French toast—witnessed the man who toasted him in Sumerian using a south Erek accent, but who had been dead for many years.

Today Tom is known as the best French toast maker in the world.

Although his mother passed away years ago, he used his Pear After Life (PAL) cell phone to call her. "Ma, I made it. Fantastic. Best French toast ever."

"Glad to hear it, my son," she answered. "You never gave up. That's good."

"How's it going up there?"

"It's quiet, though I'm adjusting."

"Any words of encouragement from your perspective?"

"Well, my advice from here is: If you want to do something, never give up. Up here, the Big Boss speaks to us every morning, gives us a pep talk. He has a longer perspective, and He says the same thing. 'Even if it takes an eternity, never give up.'"

"Sounds good, Ma. I like it."

"Yes, and I can tell you, because I have a good perspective from here. Time is an illusion. Everything of importance really lasts forever. The paltry, stupid, unimportant stuff falls away and disappears, proving how worthless it really was to begin with. It shows you how many are willing, and how important it is, to wait for a good piece of French toast."

"Yes, Ma, it took a while. As you told me when I wanted to become a cook at age nine, 'A mix of patience and hard work with eggs and batter are the ingredients for successful French toast.'"

"How did you organize it and put it all together? How did you finally do it?"

"It's totally opposite to the way I used to cook. But the old approach never worked. My excitement, enthusiasm, exhilaration have always been suppressed, *drained* out of cuisine, and especially by French toast batter, through the fear of making mistakes, not cooking perfectly, being compared to the pros and great chefs of the past. It was a fear-based approach. All my life, my self-image was that I couldn't cook, especially French toast!

"But that's all over. Now I can!"

His mother savored her happiness. "Wonderful," she finally said. "You're a smart, earthly lad. How do you explain it?"

"Index finger pointed the way."

Such Dreams Conquer the World

PAPA JONES SAT IN WONDER before the sun. Why was it shining so magnificently that morning? Not a cloud in sight. Perfect temperature. A slight breeze blowing. Zephyr of happiness, easy and gentle, helping to create such a beautiful day.

He sat on his porch in awe.

Then he saw his neighbor, Duane Dualism, crossing the street to visit him.

"Good morning, Mr. Jones," said Duane, tipping his black- and-white hat. "I see by the smile on your face and the shine in your eyes that you're feeling wonderful." Dualism pulled on his suspender and snapped it. "What's the matter?"

Jones stiffened in defense. "Nothing's the matter, you fool," he answered. "Everything is fine."

"That's what you'd like to think," Duane countered, "but as you know from your lessons in Greek polytheistic philosophy, something is always wrong."

"I only read *mono*theistic books," Jones declared. "Besides, Plato only wrote about the *idea* of being wrong, not its actuality. What would be the matter, anyhow?"

"It's a beautiful day, that's what's the matter."

"You're crazy. What's wrong with a beautiful day?"

"It makes you forget your *purpose*," Duane explained. "You must always move toward a magnificent goal. Otherwise you get depressed."

Jones blinked. ". . . How do you know that about me?"

"I observe you every day from my house across the street. My windows give me a good view and perspective. When people face you directly, they can often see you better than you can see yourself."

"You mean you watch my moods from a distance?"

"Yes. From the first floor, I get a realistic view. And from the *second* floor, I can peer into your brain—your moods, your thoughts, even your dreams."

"I didn't know that. Do you see dualism in my mind again? Maybe you came for another reason. Is it time for our session?"

Dualism nodded.

Jones rose from his chair and lied down on the porch.

His neighbor stood over him and waved his magic finger. "Let the therapy begin."

A hypnotic cloak slowly descended upon Jones. Soon, with Duane hovering over him and ready to listen, he entered the deep recesses of his mind.

At first, only grunts emerged from his mouth. Then, actual words began to form, followed by complete sentences.

"Realistic goals are fine," he muttered, "but I also need unrealistic, unattainable goals. I want to glow, move, nay speed toward the shining light. Though such lightning travels may fill me with dread, they absorb my mind and, in a strange way, make me happy."

Duane smiled, and stroked the semicircular canal in Jones' left ear. "Go on," he purred.

"Although periods of rest and ecstasy are part of my trip, these ephemeral blips are only *moments*. When new struggles emerge, my dual nature—revolutionary and accepting, resistant and happy, negative and positive—will help me conquer them."

Duane smiled in satisfaction. His teeth shone in the sun. "Dream on, my friend," he said. "Such dreams conquer the world."

A Little Better

"DO IT A LITTLE DIFFERENT and better each time. Those are the rules." That's what Big Mama Lotion said after cooking breakfast. "And these rules hold for any age. From six to eighty, four to ninety, two to one hundred. Age doesn't matter. Rules of life are the same."

Marcel swallowed his oatmeal. "What about the ladder of fame?" he asked. "I want to be known and famous."

"You mean ladder of wisdom. Fame and famous is short-term, lower rungs on the wisdom ladder. 'All Is One' is at the top."

"Hmm," Marcel considered this as he stirred his oatmeal.

Mama continued. "If you combine short-term with All Is One, you end up with 'All Is Short,' or 'Many Is One.' At the top of the ladder, it doesn't matter anymore. There, on the highest level, short is long, many is few, one is all, and all is one."

"Pretty good." Marcel took another spoonful. "You're smart."

Mama Lotion nodded in agreement and untied her apron. "This shows how, in the long run, differences and distinctions, groupings and differentiation are only for sissies. True believers live beyond this cowardice. They believe in no difference, no distinction, no groupings, no differentiation."

"A wise lecture, Mama. I'll take your wisdom to the grave."

"Not so fast, my son. First, you still have to do the laundry and take out the garbage."

Slow Wise Notes

NOTHING STICKS," COMPLAINED SEYMOUR WISENOTE, leading child of the Soflat family. "Like life itself, all passes through me."

"And yet one needs goals to survive," Grandma claimed. Seymour watched smoke from her ancient wisdom and history rising to the ceiling. "Without them, one falls into the black abyss of cosmic meaninglessness. And that's no place for a good Jewish boy to be."

"I agree, Grandma. But where else is there to go? That is the nature of life itself."

"True. But just because long-range truth hits you on the head is no reason to submit. Never give in to this so-called truth. Knock it on the head, beat it, smash it, kill it, do whatever you need to survive it. It is mere fashion and often serves as an excuse to do nothing. Besides, there is always *so-called* truth and truth itself. So-called truth visits during moments of desperation. Pay no attention to this phantom. Like passing thunder bursting over your head, it may seem very real at the moment, but just wait awhile. Soon the bugger passes and a fresh sunny sky will appear. That is the *real* truth, the one you want to remember and embrace. The sun lasts forever. Clouds come and go."

"That sounds so good, wise, Grandma. But who can believe it? We weak mortals succumb daily to cloud formations. What chance do we have in the rain?"

"Kick the buggers! That's what I say. Never give in! Keep the cutting sword of goals straight in front of you. Attitude wins every fight—even if you lose!"

Seymour wasn't convinced. "How can you be so certain, especially in this uncertain world?"

"Everybody needs a skeleton. And every skeleton needs a body."

". . . What kind of answer is that?"

"Support is vital in this transient world. Goals are your support team. If no one gives you one, create it yourself."

"I like team sports."

"Then go for it."

Moods

MR. FARSWELL JONES WOKE UP with knee pain in the morning. He worried, drank his coffee, and started studying Romanian history. He moved on to grammar, read a bit about Romanian prepositions and etymology, and even researched the Latin roots of the Romanian words "cu" (with) and "lapte" (milk).

Forty minutes later, he felt energized, inspired, and ready to roll. Yet nothing had actually happened. Only his mood had changed.

His wife walked in for breakfast. He told her about the roller-coaster mood phenomenon.

An expert in human psychology and Buddhist philosophy, she said, "One thing you can't trust is your moods."

Jones took another sip of coffee. In a hopeful voice, he said, "If only I could learn that."

Rage

SNORTING, SHE GRABBED THE ARMCHAIR and tore off the fabric with her bare hands. She squeezed the stuffing out of the pillow and stomped on the armchair frame, quickly turning it into a heap of smashed wood and splinters. Without bothering to open the window, she hurled the sofa through it.

Shattered glass flew in all directions.

"I hate this house!" she yelled, driving her foot through the plaster wall. "I can't stand looking at *you*, either!" she screamed at her husband, who was hiding in the corner. Grabbing him by the scruff of the neck, she crumpled his starched collar. It sent his shirt buttons flying in all directions.

"Estelle, you're overreacting" were the last words he uttered before she heaved him across the lawn into the rose bushes.

"I can't stand the smell of those roses either," she

shouted as she started tearing out the bushes and ploughing them under with her heel.

Finally, her rage subsided. She found a pear in the refrigerator and sat in the corner munching it, while all the paintings on the wall hung trembling from their hooks.

Moving to France

A LOUSE BIT HIS FINGERTIP as Neanderthal Dan walked along Nohome Road, heading for his cave dwelling high in Minusland.

What could save him from Great Down feeling? On the other hand, should he *be* saved? Why bother in the first place?

Mama Neanderthal rolled down from her bed high in the Andes. In a flower-perfumed voice bred from years of plant gathering, she asked him, "Where are you going, my child?"

"I'm feeling down, Mama. I'm lost. I'll walk on Nohome Road until I find myself."

"My darling, no need to cringe. Down is often a good place to be. And it's not as bad as it looks. After all, down is the prelude to up. A decent, healthy descent eventually leads to a a lovely ascent. Down is the way to go up. Twin trails in disguise, Janus-faced directions foretelling a new year. Descend far enough, and you'll reach Ascent Trail."

Neanderthal Dan scratched his head, pulled a louse from his hair and, in awe, replied, "I will consider your words, Mama. What does Papa Neanderthal say?"

"Papa is asleep in his cave. He doesn't do directions."

"But he likes hunting. He must have something to say about place and purpose."

"That's true. But he has a masculine approach. Your father believes in infinite rising. In his view, this comes only after beating the ups and downs, conquering conflicts and moving beyond them."

"Has he ever done that?"

"Oh, yes, he did it years ago. These days, though, after hunting, he sleeps most of the time."

"Sleeps?"

"Well, not exactly sleep. It *seems* like he's asleep, but actually it's not a *real* sleep. Most of the time he sits or lies in his cave, performing Neanderthal meditation."

"Is that a performing art?"

"Yes, but he only does it for Ha Shemovar, our Neanderthal Antler god."

"I thought he only loved deer. You mean he worships something above the trees?"

"Yes, but it's a secret. He doesn't want our Neanderthal brethren to know."

"What about our Neanderthal sisters?"

"There are no sisters, only brethren. Sisters belong to our brethren."

"Aha. Very Neanderthal. Nice to know. Are all Neanderthals earthbound?"

"At the moment, yes. But your father hopes to change that. Through the power of Antler meditation, he wants to point all Neanderthals to a higher reality. One day, we will all hunt on the Reindeer Road together."

"That is a worthy cause. I'm proud of Papa." Neanderthal Dan scratched his head. After removing a few more lice, he asked, "Is there any way I can help?"

"Of course. Remember how near-sighted you used to be? Well, we gave you that pair of Neomillenium glasses as a day-birth present. Through them you said you saw chickens and pieces of the future. The glasses also helped you penetrate the illusion of travel on Nohome Road. You felt free and whole when you wore them. That's what Antler meditation is all about. So wear your glasses. They help a lot."

"But, Ma, I enjoy illusions."

"I know you do."

"I wouldn't be a Neanderthal without them."

"That's true. But someday we plan to move to a cave in France."

"France? Where is that?"

"In a dream of the future."

"Thanks, Ma."

Perhaps You're Right

"Perhaps," said Martha with a definitiveness well beyond maybe, "you're being visited by travel demons."

Sam threw back his head and laughed. "You must be kidding. Why should those creatures affect me? Am I not Sam the Fruit Man?"

"Indeed, you are. But even the best fruit can rot, especially if it's attacked by *touriosis nemicosis.*"

"Market madness, Martha. I won't give in to it! Stay strong and intellectual. That's what my mother always said."

"But she was always wrong."

At that moment, Sam heard a knock on his door. Before him stood his testy neighbor, Emily Emoticon. She smiled with neighborly assurance and handed him a pink slip. "Sam, your

anxiety test scores were too low. You're fired." Softening her voice, she went on. "It's true, we need frightened people in our company, but you are simply not one of them. You don't fit in, don't belong." Singing an ancient Roman martial anxiety song in original Latin, she turned and disappeared down the street.

Sam didn't know what to do. Should he return to the old neighborhood of Less Terre, where he had dwelt in anxious peace and unhappy comfort? Or should he remain in his new purchased residence, the stately quasi-mansion he had acquired through years of heartbreaking labor in the anxiety field? Since he moved into Plus Heights, the brave northern quarter of the city, his fear faculties, along with his ancient anxieties, had disappeared.

Backing his mind into a corner, he sat down on his Bloomingdale's hardwood conference chair to discuss the pros and cons with himself. "Can I dwell in security and be happy? Or is living with anxiety more comfortable?" He considered the conflict. Hours passed. "Maybe there's a compromise solution where I can do both—security and anxiety as one. I like *that*!"

Sam pondered further. "I don't want to *reject* Emily, but I want to move beyond her as well. Is there a new neighborhood where Angela Anxiety, Fanny Fear, Karen Comfort, and Henrietta Happiness all live together in peace and harmony? Or do I have too many female friends? And what about daring, diving, confidence, and masculinity? What about my *male* friends?"

Martha listened. Stroking her chin, she declared, "These questions can only be answered in Spanish. Perhaps you'll find them in Cuba."

"There you go with 'perhaps' again."

"Perhaps you're right. Nevertheless, why not ask Fidel Castro, after you arrive?"

"Is he still alive?"

"I'm not sure. But does that really matter?"

Waiting for the Mail

I SURE HOPE I GET SOME MAIL TOMORROW," Lance said as he fed his pigs. He shoveled slop into their trough and continued to glance at page 63 of Ovid's *Metamorphosis*. Holding the book open with the heel of his work boot and letting the sun illuminate the text, he began reading the luxuriant hexameters. How he loved Latin! Every morning before feeding his pigs, he sat at his desk under the cozy light of his table lamp. Coffee in hand, he spent a meditative hour poring over each word, looking up meanings in his Latin dictionary, then checking with Webster's for any Indo-European roots or connections between ancient and modern tongues. Lance believed a thorough understanding of etymology not only enriched his life but provided the insights required to run a successful pig farm.

Not that his farm was successful. Far from it. Pigs often died, especially when he wanted them to produce beef. His feeding methods, although innovative, were also questionable, for when he ran out of corn meal and slop, he tore pages from Dante's *Inferno*, and threw them into the trough.

One morning, he was crossing his farmyard, pondering important problems as he stroked his chin. On the right stood his favorite pen. He kept asking himself, was he wasting his life as a pig farmer? Should he become a Latin scholar?

He squatted beside a sleeping hog. "Tell me," he demanded, "what is more worthy? To place pork chops and ham on the dinner tables of distant city folks, or to study Virgil and read Cicero in the original?"

The pig snorted, grunted, wiggled its ear, and turned over. Its snout widened. In a low, rumbling voice, it replied, "Lance, I'd think it over a bit more. Mid-life changes take time." It snorted again before closing its eyes and burying its snout in the mud.

"You think so?" Lance replied. "But what do you know? You're only a hog. Besides, I work by consensus. I'll ask the others." He trudged across the pen. "Trouble is, I feel foolish asking pigs for answers," he grumbled. "They're not as smart as they look. What do they know of life beyond the pen? Better for me to leave this farm, see the world, expand my horizons, and become a credit to the human race. Besides, I want to read Virgil in the original."

So, he made plans. The very quest that had convinced him to buy his pig farm was now pulling him away from the security of his pens and propelling him into the world of men, women, dogs, and commerce. But would he be able to study Latin or read Virgil and Ovid in such a world?

On Tuesday morning, he packed his suitcase, left the farm in the care of his aged parents, locked his front door, and marched down the country road.

Soon he passed a farmhouse. An old man was sitting on a rocker on the front porch. Lance had seen old men, but this one was older by far. He drew closer to look him over: torn shirt, baggy overalls, gnarled fingers, white beard. "Who are you?" he asked.

"I am the god of tooth-fillings," the old man told him.

"My teeth are fine," Lance said," but my life is full of holes. How did you sleep last night?"

"I never sleep," the old man answered. "I watch the stars. My cousin was a star. So was my uncle. I was one too, I think. Now I'm a professional Old Man. I make house calls, visit hospitals, pick up the mail."

"I don't get mail," Lance complained. "People only write to my pigs."

"Hire me," the Old Man advised. "You'll see mail pile up to your ceiling." He hitched up his suspenders. "Tell me, son, why do you want to get mail?"

"I'm looking for a goal," Lance answered. "Maybe I can find it in the mail."

"You need a commitment, son." The Old Man raised his arm, swatted Lance across the face, and sent the pig farmer flying off the porch.

"What the hell'd you do that for?" Lance yelled when he got up.

"I want you to pay attention to your pigs, son."

Lance rubbed his chin. "I feel like punching you in the

mouth."

"I wouldn't do that, son."

Lance clenched his fist. "Okay. What do you have to teach me, then?"

"I already did," the Old Man replied. "But there's more. Go back to your pigs. Wait for the next mail. It's coming tomorrow."

Where the Wild Mind Dwells

D ARE I EVEN WRITE A WORD?" ASKED SAM. "Don't you miss your wild vision?" answered Mama Loschen.

Sam pondered that. "Yes, I do. But right now, I can hardly see straight, and my brain is dropping key words into the garbage bin of forgetfulness. There must be a solution to such a problem."

Mama Loschen leaned on her thinking stick. Her wide body, heavy with thought, folded easily over her even wider stomach. "Indeed, my son, there is. But I'm not giving it to you. I hate this house, and until I can move, I'm not giving you or anyone else a thing. Besides, if I did, it would be cheap, and your current sieve of a mind would easily forget it. Better to suffer quietly on your own. Pain will recalibrate your brain, and eventually a new, vital personality will pop out. That's what pregnancy is all about."

"Is that why you're so fat, Mama?"

"Of course. Mamas are always fat."

"You wouldn't be referring to *saturated* fats—"

Mama whacked Sam over his coolidge. "No, silly boy, those fats destroy both mind and body. I'm speaking about warm, vital, energy-producing fats, hot fats that will build up your habit-cooled mind. That's why I whacked you over your coolidge—to warm you up, heat a few of your latent silly parts. You've become stiff and lame. Your funny brain has retreated into the dark corners. I haven't heard a joke or pun for months."

Sam shrank into a corner. Finally, he emerged and asked, "If I find this funny mind in my hidden closet, what will I do with it?"

"Many things."

"Like what? And what about public consumption, love and acceptance? Why bother writing again if this will never happen? I don't have the interest, passion, or energy to *promote* my writing. This is hardly an attitude with which to pursue fame, acceptance, or fortune. I know my publication attitude stinks. I'm floundering in total discouragement. No one loves me, and no one loves my work. They don't even read it! What about that?"

Mama Loschen answered in dulcet tones, "Start with your own heart. Never mind the public—at least, not yet. Here's a beginning question: Where does your wild music dwell?"

The question stunned Sam. He sank to the floor, lay on his mother's rug of rumination for a while. Visions of storm clouds, wild rains, and happy sunsets brewed in his mind. Finally, he rose. "Does wild mind follow wild music," he asked, "or is wild music born in wild mind?"

"They are twins. It really doesn't matter who started what, or even where they are born. They are born to exist. And to be used by you!"

"Who will be the leader? My wild mind or me?"

"Your wild mind *is* you! Be true to yourself. As for the public, you'll eventually find your fans, and they will follow."

YEARS LATER, SARAH BOSWICK BOUGHT three copies of Sam's first self-published novel, *Where the Wild Mind Dwells*. Two were used as coffee coasters on her living room table.

A month later, after reading the third copy, she placed it, along with other novels and self-help books, on the sidewalk outside her home. Her neighbor, Lace Hodkins, picked it up, passed it on to his son, Bob Hodkins, president of Universal Publishers. Bob loved the book, called Sam, and offered him a contract. Years later, while vacationing on the profits of his best seller, Sam was able to purchase a new home for his mother.

Does Soaring Make You Sore? Or Vice Versa?

WHEN TOM SUFFERED FROM WRITING SORES, red marks appeared on his back. Soon they spread to his hands, arms, and legs. One morning, they appeared on his face! Unsightly.

"I can't stand looking at you," his girlfriend, Irene, complained. "You've become ugly. What will my friends say? My mother will never accept you. Neither will my father or the rest of the family. How can we get married? You've been getting worse for a long time. You're a disgrace. I've tolerated these imperfections for months only because they were invisible to others. But now that your writing sores are appearing in public, I can't stand it any longer. I'm leaving you, and I won't come back until you fix your problem!"

This abandonment mortified Tom. But the writing sores, especially the blotches peppering his face, bothered him even more.

He needed a medical appointment, and he needed it fast.

Who can cure writing sores? he asked himself. What kind of doctor treats writing patients?

A Google search turned up nothing. In total frustration, he decided to ask his wise neighbor, Dr. Iyam Wiesekorper.

On Sunday, Tom knocked on his door. The good doctor appeared.

"Good morning, Iyam," Tom said. "I need your help. I'm suffering from writing sores."

"Ah, I can see that," said the good doctor. "Come in. Sit down on the living room sofa." Wiesekorper pulled up a chair, sat opposite his neighbor, surveyed his face, and looked wisely into his eyes.

"I see blots of frustration and ignorance on your face. But most important, Tom, I see the hidden panic of Muse abandonment." Wiesekorper paused a moment. "Tom, your blemishes are large. However, I have good news for you: You only have a spelling problem! *You have misspelled the word 'sore.'* Change your spelling from 'sore' to 'soar,' and your face will clear up. Your mind will be free. Your sores will disappear."

"Wow! Is it really that simple?"

"Yes."

Tom sat there, stunned.

"Words affect your vitals," said Weisekorper. "They influence your well-being. I know writing is difficult, frustrating, even painful, and it can therefore make you sore. But you listen to me—change the spelling, and you'll be okay."

"Simple as that?"

"Simple as that."

In deep appreciation, Tom shook his hand and kissed the floor beneath the doctor's feet.

He went home, sat down in front of his keyboard, and cried, "Abandon sores!" Soon, a few words sputtered out. Then, hour after hour, he sat in front of the screen as words poured through his fingers. When each appeared, a red sore vanished from his face. He let his imagination fly through space and time, creating whole paragraphs as more sores vanished.

After hours of soaring at his keyboard, he had had enough. And his sores were gone!

Simple as that?

Simple as that.

And when Tom got up, only his backside felt sore.

What Are Friends For?

TOM WAS SUFFERING FROM WRITER'S BLOCK. I think a visit to Jack's house will relax me, he thought. Jack lived on the other side of town, and since Tom needed exercise, he walked.

On the way, he passed trees, houses, children playing, a tunnel, and a truck.

Finally, he saw Jack's place up ahead. And a magnificent house it was: Beautiful shutters hung from each rectangular window; a bright red brick facade shone in the afternoon sunlight; a slate roof crowned the wide second floor; and white smoke was rising from the tall, majestic chimney.

Then Tom noticed that smoke was also coming out of the windows. He saw even more smoke creeping from the sides and bottom of the front door. Jack's house was on fire!

He shoved open the front door and rushed into the living room. He ran down the hallway until he found Jack in the bedroom, suffocating from smoke and coughing out his guts.

Dragging him by the hand and collar, he managed to get him out just as the roof collapsed behind them.

"That was a close call," gasped Jack, sitting on the front lawn. "Thanks for saving my life." He brushed sweat from his forehead. "But am I worth saving? I've been so down ever since my novel was rejected for the sixteenth time. I appreciate your effort, but it would have been better to save the sofa."

"Cut it out, Jack!" cried Tom as the last wall slumped into rubble behind them. "Any life is worth saving, especially a friend's . . . How did it happen, anyway?"

"When you hear the reason, you'll know I'm a true friend," Jack replied as fire engines came screaming down the street. "I lit it. I love the sound, the smell, the warmth of a fire. And the reason I lit this one is—" Jack gasped for air again "—is to give you a subject to write about for your next story! I did it for you, Tom, I did it for you!" As he uttered this last, he collapsed to the ground.

"What a friend," said Tom with admiration.

At that moment the fire captain told his men not to bother throwing water on the house.

Tom turned away from the fire engines and started up the block. Glancing back, he said, "The embers from Jack's house will glow in my mind forever. I'll dedicate my next story to him."

Do What You're Told!

HECTOR MARTINEZ, A NUTRITIONAL RESEARCHER, received a letter from Jack Splat, president of Lemon Makers, Inc.:

"Dear Mr. Martinez, our company is the first to attempt the impossible: We want to turn our lemon peels into fruit. How can this be done? We'd like to hire you, with your nutritional expertise to see if you can figure out how these peels can be transformed into fruit. Are you interested?"

Hector, who had been unemployed for six months, grabbed the job.

After working in the Lemon Makers lab for a week, stymied and frustrated, he put in a call to his Aristotelean Logic/Platonic Idealism Club president, Mary Funnel. "Are you free after work?"

Mary stuffed meditation directions into her pocket and checked the schedule pinned above her desk. "Why do you ask?"

"I'm not making any headway on this lemon project."

"That often happens with you. Is it urgent?"

"Yes. The lemons are recalcitrant and stiff. So are the peels. Not easy working with them. But I'm also beginning to feel the project itself is morally wrong. I'm in need of spiritual guidance." He paused to let the seriousness of his emotional state sink in.

Mary worked across the street, pressing pants and shirts for Merlin's Custom Shirts and Suits. "I've got two appointments with Merlin managers this afternoon," she said. "But I can juggle them around. So yes, I can make it."

"Great." Hector watched a sparrow fly past his window on its way to a branch. "Let's meet after work in Monaghan's Ail and Healing House Bar for a drink."

Mary sounded pleased. "Okay, great. I like Monaghan's. And don't worry. I'll bring my solving iron. We'll press out this crease."

"Thanks, Mary. You're a good friend."

That evening, they sat down together at the bar. After nibbling at a pretzel and a few potato chips, Mary took a sip of her martini and looked him in the eye. "What's happening, Hector?"

Downcast and forlorn, he glanced at his shoes. "The Lord told me to shut up!"

"Again?" Mary shook her head in exasperation. "Did He say anything else this time?"

"He mumbled something like 'Bey sim ha.' Throaty, guttural, deep."

"What's that supposed to mean?"

"Hard to say. I listened some more. The Hebrew seemed to turn into English. What I finally understood was: "Serve me with joy . . . or else!"

"Or else what?"

"I'm not sure." Hector paused, trying to recall the conversation. "First it got quiet. Then I heard the sound of thunder, and a voice commanded, 'Use my dopamine release program.'"

Mary leaned forward, intrigued. "A heavenly drug program. How do you do it?"

"I don't know. I heard only silence after that."

Mary's admiring eyes widened. "You're quite a theologian, Hector. Silence is a good teacher. Can you maybe expound a bit on this loving doctrine?"

Tapping his beer glass with a pencil, he pondered the question. Minutes passed. Mary became impatient. "At least tell me where can you find such a program."

He clamped a bony finger across his jaw and let the digit wander into his mouth and touch the back of his tongue, hoping to release his deepest visceral idea.

"I *don't know*," he finally gagged. "But I *can* tell you I feel a deep internal pressure to enjoy myself. I hate pressure, especially such an extreme one. Do I really *have to* enjoy myself? Why can't I be miserable, like the rest of my friends?"

Mary took another sip of her martini. "Misery is good," she said. "But as Father Berrybut said in his last sermon, joy is better. Without it, you're not really worshiping."

Hector rubbed his patella. "I pray my knee pain gets

better, but so far no luck. I don't find that prayer very joyful."

"Maybe it's time to kneel with a pad. Or change your prayer position. Max Lotus worships standing on his head; Guru Saul prays in the full lotus position, and Roland Glatt, the rifle salesman, is not only kosher, but prays by focusing his gun on pound cake. There are lots of ways to pray for what you like."

"You mean I've got to practice?"

"Yes. It's a discipline."

"Enjoyment is a discipline?"

"Absolutely. The Lord is telling you to express yourself and have joy in the process. A tough commandment. But mucho worthy."

"I see you're using some Spanish."

"Of course. God is Spanish."

"I thought He was Hebrew."

"He's all things. But that's too grand, too universal for now. Let's stick with you."

"You mean I must force my mind into a slot? I *have to* enjoy myself?"

"Damn right. It's a commandment. You heard what the Lord said."

"What a downer."

Mary grabbed Hector by the scruff of the neck and shook him hard. "You're lucky the Lord speaks to you. He even gave you directions! So just follow your orders and shut up! Joy is tough. But since it's a commandment, do what you're told."

Hector sat silently and let the clobbering settle in his mind. "Maybe you're right," he finally said.

Mary kicked his bar stool with friendly force. "Now get out of here," she said. "Walk that road and shut up!"

Hector went to his car, and Mary headed home for another martini.

The next morning, Hector's alarm clock sounded like a knock on his door. Shaking his head as he rose from a deep dreamy sleep, he rolled out of bed, put on his safari giraffe bathrobe and stumbled across the floor.

"Who is it?" he called.

The voice outside his apartment sounded raspy and hollow, but commanding and mature as well. "Message for Hector Martinez."

Hector opened the door. Before him stood a short man in a blue uniform, whose withered face reminded him of a Pathmark chicken. The mailman's hunched-over shoulders and clucking voice added to his fowl look. He wore a blue cap which said "Messenger."

"Hello, Mr. Martinez. I'm with Cockburn Messenger Service. We have a letter bomb for you."

Hector jumped back.

"No, no," shouted the mailman. "Not that kind. The purpose of this letter is to explode and expand your mind."

Hector quieted down. He checked out the messenger again, this time looking deep into his eyes. Surprised by the calm in the messenger's aqueous humour, he imagined a Garden of Eden deep behind the cornea.

"Who's it from?"

The mailman turned the letter over in his hands. "No return address. But we know the letter is important because of its weight."

"Okay, I'll take it. Where do I sign?"

The mailman held up his palm. "Sign here."

Although an experienced, semi-professional palm reader, Hector had never seen such a hand before. He took it in his, turned it upright, and examined palmedic landscape. "That's quite a life line you've got," he said in admiration.

"Thank you," said the mailman in a humble voice. "I got it from my father."

"Oh? Where does he live?"

"With my mother."

"Any brothers or sisters?"

"I'm the only son."

"Aha, that explains it. Only children live longer."

The mailman drew back. Suddenly, his face reddened, twisting with pain and rage. "How dare you cross-examine me," he roared. "My family is sacrosanct." Then, just as quickly, his anger and hurt subsided. Returning to his humble voice, he said, "But never mind me. Tell me, how is *your* life?"

On guard and a bit defensive, Hector shot back, "What are you, some kind of delivery psychologist? How dare you examine me! You're just a post office messenger!"

"Post office? Ha! That miserable, feckless place. I don't work for them. I never would. I'm from a better service."

"Oh, and what is that?"

Hector hesitated, but then recognized a fleshy spot of

sympathetic listening in the messenger's right ear. Here was another chance for him to talk about the miseries of life and his Lemon problem.

"Well," Hector ventured, "things are hard. I've got a new job and I'm not handling it very well."

"At Lemon Makers, Inc.?"

Hector jaw dropped. "How do you know?"

"We messengers know a lot. We do research before each delivery. What's the problem?"

"I can't figure out how to turn lemon peels into fruit."

The messenger smiled. "That's *easy*. No problem."

"Really?"

"Yes, I do it every day."

Hector's astonishment now turned into hope. "How?"

"First, remove the dull from each peel."

"What's that? The rind?"

"No, no, the deadness. The flat, lifeless parts. You need to put the spring, jump, relish, and joy back into those peels."

"How do you do *that*?"

The messenger reached into his pocket and pulled out a vial of fluid. "This comes from Higher Sources, Inc., the company I work for. Inject each peel with this blue S-and-M dye. Some think it creates sadomasochistic tendencies, but it actually stands for Surprise and Mystery."

"And this will turn peels into fruit?"

"Absolutely. It fills each peel with amusement, wonder, and amazement. Suddenly, everyone wants to eat it. Wonder and awe are the way to go."

"But wouldn't dye injections make awful lemons?"

"Awe-*filled* is the correct word."

Hector envisioned the proper spelling in his mind. "I could use some of that. How do you do it?"

"Remember this: When it becomes fun, it becomes one."

"What's that supposed to mean?"

"When you remember the mystery and adventure of life, it becomes fun. The dull and unappealing transform into fascinating and child-like wonder. Life moves from dull and routine to amazing. Or, as we say in the business, from un-a-peeling to appealing, from dull to sparkling, from discarded rot to succulent fruit."

"Easier said than done."

"True, but possible."

"How do I start?"

The messenger pondered the question, turning its contrasting heavy and heavenly aspects over in his mind. Hector used palm-reading skills to perceive the profundity of this aspect weighing. Then the messenger invited himself into Hector's apartment, sat down on the sofa, had a cup of coffee, looked around the room at the artwork on the walls and the hand-crafted kitchen utensils, before answering. "Good question." A long pause followed while he looked around the room, checking Hector's bookshelves, lined with books on the history of lemons, chemical peel analysis, company management policies, and a Spanish dictionary.

"Dive into the research, Hector."

"You know my name?"

The messenger paid no attention to this trivial distraction. "The *fun* is in the *fruit*. Become one with the core. Peels are part of the fruit. It's all in the vision. When mystery and adventure are united, inner and outer joined together, all becomes one."

Hector absorbed this new idea in silence. The fog in his brain began to dissipate. "All in the vision, eh? I think you've nailed it."

"Nails are the way to go, especially when you're ready to sink your idea into material reality."

Relief and relaxation entered Hector's mind. "Thanks so much," he said. "I feel hopeful and much better . . . Perhaps we can meet again." He extended his hand. "What's your name?"

"I'm Freddie Lord."

"Seems I've heard that name before. Do you have an address?"

"Our house is in Beyond-the-Clouds. It's in another state. I live there with my father. Perhaps you know him. We're a family business."

"How would I know him?"

"Only in subtle ways. We don't advertise much, especially here in New Jersey. We try to keep our name secret to avoid competition."

"Well, thanks, Freddie. I really appreciate your service. Do you want a recommendation or even a commission from Lemon Makers, Inc.? I could ask our plant boss."

Freddie rose. "We don't allow recommendations," he said as he headed for the door.

"Really?"

"But we appreciate discoveries."

". . . What is that supposed to mean?"

The next day, Hector went back to work. When he sat down at his desk, although the peels and lemons that lay before him still looked separate, somehow their distance between each other did not worry, annoy, or bother him. Today, in a strange way, they all seemed to fit together. He blinked. Was it his imagination? He rose, paced the floor, checked the production of the Mona Lisa on the wall, visited the toilet, polished his glasses, returned to his desk, and looked again. Yes, somehow they still fit together, unified in a grand effort of fruit togetherness. Hector scratched his head. Was he imagining things? Probably. But what else is there but imagination? The world exists in imagination, and in his imagination Hector now felt calm, easy, satisfied, and happy.

The following Wednesday, he heard a knock on his office door.

When he opened it, his boss Jack Splat stood before him, a big smile on his face. "Good morning, Hector. You're doing a great job. Business is booming; lemons are rising. And you're getting a raise!"

Two weeks later, Jack Splat invited Hector for lunch. Over a tuna-and-rye sandwich, the boss said he was leaving the company to retire in Florida. Would Hector like to take over, manage it? Even buy it?

During the following years, Hector get more raises. Eventually, he bought the company, and slowly became a millionaire.

One day, during a monthly meeting with Mary, he felt overwhelmed with a desire to read Plato in ancient Greek and Hegel in the original German. He sold his company and retired to Lemon Island in the Caribbean, where today you can find him sitting in a lawn chair, eating fruit.

Miss Spelling

THE VOLCANIC ERUPTIONS CREATED by years of misspelling Spanish culminated in Juan Fernandez's misspelling "*acontecimiento.*" That's when he fell off the ladder, broke his front tooth on the sofa, spent big money on dental bills, and shrank his bank account to zero.

His inability to spell correctly brought nightmare visions of Orthographic Arnie, the spell devil, riding across the sheets.

Juan began to increase his Hebrew studies to improve his spelling, but that didn't work. He added Bulgarian, Hungarian, Albanian, Polish, Serbian, and bits of Arabic. Soon he had increased his internal pressure to the breaking point. When his landlady, Mrs. Delaruso, wandered into his apartment speaking Portuguese, he panicked, ran out the door, and visited his mother.

The lad wanted to release himself. But by then, as a thirty-three-year old, he had lost his infant vision.

How could he retrieve the pristine consciousness of that distant world?

For advice, he decided to ask his father-out-law, Sidney.

Sitting in shorts and a jacket by his mansion pool filled with bags of money, the wealthy iron-ore magnate turned toward his genealogical heir and planted a kiss his forehead.

"How are you, my lad?" he barked in a stellar voice radiating its usual aura of triumph. "Why do you come to Papa? Do you wish to pluck one of my wealth bags? Or is there a higher, spiritual purpose to your visit?"

"The latter," said Juan. "I come for your wisdom."

"My wisdom is free. And I sense from your hunched-up posture that you have a poor living situation."

"Correct, Uncle. Where to begin? As you know, I am no longer a child. I'm ready to leave home and enter the world. But how? What will I do to live?"

Sidney beckoned to his housekeeper, Mary Juana, who brought him his pot stick. After a restorative inhalation, he asked Juan, "What does your mother say?"

"I no longer speak to her."

"You sound angry."

"I am. Last time I visited my parents, I couldn't even spell the name of their *street* correctly. I'm getting worse and worse."

"Juan, you are wasting your rage."

". . . *Wasting*?"

"Uh-huh."

"I don't *like* waste."

"That's a good sign." Sidney patted his cheek. "You

have no reason to worry, my lad. I'm here to change your path. *That* is why you came today."

Downcast and forlorn, Juan studied a busy ant crawling over a blade of grass. His voice sank deeper in his throat as he grumbled, "Yes Uncle, my Spanish and all my other linguistic projects have lost their sparkle. I've gone as far as I can go. It feels like the molecules in my brain are menstruating and the cells are evolving into what, I don't know. My blood flow has slowed to a trickle. I sit in boredom with my books. I'm dried up, scared, and only worry about spelling. What should I do?"

"My boy, you're suffering from dry-brain syndrome, a common malady in this modern world. To reconnect with your energy source, drink lots of water."

". . . Water?"

"Water encourages the flow of words. Obviously, you've run dry. Your brain has become a midbar of Hebrew supplicants."

Juan stiffened. "I don't want to spend forty years in any desert."

"Then it's time to visit Sinai."

"With water? It's so boring."

"Is Niagara Falls boring?"

Juan considered the question. "No," he admitted. "But speed is not what I'm after. And water just doesn't feel right. Too mild. After my visit to the vineyards in Mendoza, I prefer wine."

"Aha, I see your trip to Argentina was a worthwhile graduation present. But the Greek philosopher Thales pointed out that the world is *made* of water."

"Who cares what he said?"

"Well, it *could* be that the hydrogen and oxygen are too mild for you. But you still need to irrigate your brain. Maybe a Dionysian solution would be better."

"Now *there's* a Greek I can relate to."

"Precisely."

"But I still misspell words."

"Look, you may just need a new view of spelling."

"That's sweet of you, Uncle."

"Misspelling does not always equal a mistake."

Juan tilted his head wistfully. "I wish that were true, but I think you're wrong. The business world wants correct spelling and standard pronunciation. I can't spell!" he cried in desperation. "Who will *hire* me if this keeps up?"

Sidney laid a calming hand on his nephew's shoulder. "Your mother told me about your spelling worries and how you've brought these concerns to seventeen therapists in order to free yourself from the curse."

". . . She did?"

"Yes. And your complaining has its virtues. It reveals and builds an inner library of clarifying concerns. Once these are organized in a sound hierarchy, the rest is easy."

"Hah! Nothing is easy for me."

"Except complaining. Complaining is good. It leads to innovative thinking, the kind I do in my wine cellar."

"What?"

"Some call it 'whining' but I call it 'wining.' I contemplate situations over a glass of chardonnay, a sauvignon blanc, a merlot. Sometimes I use pinot or a sparkling zinfandel. It helps me remember that 'misspellings' can be the creative new workings of old, worn-out words. Often they result in the artistic production of new ones! Take the Old English saga *Beowulf*. The Vikings stole the language and turned it into Swedish. So-called 'misspellings' can be new word creations in disguise."

Juan listened in silence. "Really?"

"Of course."

"That's hopeful."

"A good start."

"I'll think about it."

"Excellent. And while you're doing that, a glass of merlot from my wine cellar can smooth the process."

Juan considered the proposal. "Why would yours be better than others?"

Sidney straightened his back and rose to his full height. "As your mother may have explained but you may not know, part of my fortune derives from oenology workshops I give all over the country. The secret to my Bottles of Happiness brand is that I play Gregorian chants twenty-four hours a day in my wine cellar. Especially "Ferment Forever," the chant written by Pope Gregory himself in 598 A.D., after his visit to a winery in Sicily. The chant makes the wine barrels dance—taking small steps, of course—and inspires grapes to ferment celestially, thus creating their heavenly taste."

Sidney led Juan into the mansion. They climbed the spiral staircase to his library, where, on a heavy bookshelf, he found Himmel von Strassel's 1968 edition of *Freude*

Zwischen den Weintraub (Joy Among the Grapes). Behind it stood an aged bottle of wine. Withdrawing a corkscrew from his vest pocket, he opened a bottle and poured some for Juan.

"You'll like this."

Juan swirled the wine in the glass and lifted it to his lips. Sidney watched his eyes disappear in pleasure behind his lids.

"Have another sip," Sidney suggested when the lids rose again.

"This tastes *sooo* good."

Sidney smiled. "My best. Only $19.95."

"Can I take it home with me?"

"Of course."

"If my spelling improves, I'll send you a check."

"You mean your misspelling."

"Well, I'll have to get a job first."

"That sounds practical, very businesslike."

Juan took another sip.

"What about my dry-brain syndrome?" he asked. "Will it go away?"

"Slowly. You've become more fluid already."

"You could be right, Uncle. I feel it already. I never thought wisdom could come in this form. Thank you."

"My pleasure. So, shall I expect a check in the mail? Do we have a deal?"

"Yes, we do."

Juan embraced his uncle. Filled with a future of new ideas, he headed home to start his new life.

The Strange Running Club

JASON WOKE IN THE MORNING feeling a deep sadness. He called it "cosmic depression." He didn't know why he felt this way every morning. Could it be the transience of life? Or the fact he had to go back to work in the law office he hated?

He consulted with himself: "Cosmic depression is a common occurrence, a given part of my daily existence. It's a *meaning* thing. Is there an answer? I know that when I dive into daily tasks, my gray veil lifts, the fog disappears, and I feel better. How strange."

Jason's self-consultations bore fruit when he realized that his daily cosmic sadness event was a *running* problem. He had posted an inferior time in his first marathon. Now he wanted to increase his speed and come in under four hours. "Bob did it in three hours and twenty-six minutes, and he's only a year older than I am," he complained to his hidden self.

"You're so competitive," was the only answer he received.

Jason admitted it was time to start seeing his running therapist, Dr. Bosley Strange, or "Marathon Mike" as his patients fondly called him.

The following Wednesday, driving in from New Jersey, Jason fought the usual traffic crossing the George Washington Bridge. But this time, instead of frustrated rage, yelling at the drivers, and cursing at the toll booth, he found that the honks and screams of other drivers acted as a stimulant for his competitive juices, a soothing mental warm-up and preparation for the struggle ahead.

After two hours of driving, he finally reached the doctor's forty-third-floor Empire State Building office. As he sat on the sofa in the waiting room, he read the inspirational aphorisms hanging in frames on the wall, attributed the Hellenic philosopher of Canarsie, Pheidipiddes Peripopolous of Brooklyn.

"Blessed are the obstacles."

"Fun is ecstasy in one syllable."

"The rewards of victory are more of the same."

Greeting his former patient at the door, Dr. Strange extended his hand. "Welcome back and forth, Jason."

Face flushed, shoulders hunched, primed and ready, Jason dashed to the red armchair and sank into its friendly leather. Brilliant sunlight streaming in through a southeast window flooded the office.

The doctor sat down in his chair, said nothing, and waited. Jason leaned back in the armchair, and drifted into his usual depression. Ten minutes later, when he began to sniffle and cry, Dr. Strange offered him a box of tissues. "Have you made any progress in your quest for higher learning?" he asked.

After an initial bout of nose-blowing, Jason coughed out, "My running stinks. I'm too slow."

Four minutes passed. The doctor answered. "Are you sure?"

Jason was suddenly energized. "What a stupid question!" he boiled. "What is the *matter* with you? Why do I even bother coming here?"

". . . You're a strange patient."

"Me? *You're* the one that's strange. Look at your *name*."

"That is true."

Jason lapsed into silence, fixing his eyes on the shadow behind the doctor's chair. A gurgle rose in his throat as he cogitated on high alert. ". . . Am I wrong? Perhaps your name *isn't* Strange. Perhaps I'm talking to myself because I *am* strange."

Dr. Strange rose from his chair to place a kindly hand on Jason's head. "Very insightful of you. Yes, I too am Strange. We are brothers under the same strange flesh."

He lit his pipe, balanced it on his ashtray, and returned to his seat. "Look, Jason, people are *all* strange. We are mirrors of strangiosity. Let's explore ours. Strange people need to stick together."

"But I don't *want* to be strange. I want to be normal."

"*That* really *is* strange. Are you sure?"

"Now you're making me doubt myself."

"Doubt is the first step toward knowledge. But let's get back to your running speed."

Jason nodded. "How can I increase my speed, especially if I doubt myself?"

Dr. Strange smiled. "We'll find out. The opposite of the strange is the known. And I *know* you can run a marathon in under four hours."

"How do you know *that?*"

"Oh, it's a fact. The bigger question is: Are facts important? And do you see them differently?"

". . . I never looked at them like that."

"Of course you didn't. Strange people don't see straight. Their vision is naturally crooked."

Dr. Strange rose again, reached into his closet, and pulled out a pair of running shoes. "Did you bring your shorts and running shoes?"

"Of course."

"Okay. Go change in the bathroom, and let's go."

The two suited runners took the elevator downstairs, and began a slow jog down Thirty-fourth Street.

They ran in silence past stores, waited at stop lights, and crossed avenues until they reached Fifty-ninth Street. By the time they ran past Columbus Circle and entered Central Park, most of Jason's daily concerns had slipped away. His unconscious, warmed and loosened by the long run, felt free to release a torrent of complaints.

His speed increased. "It's been a fuzzy year," he panted. "I've tried to maintain my marathon training, even my wandering instinct, but I've been getting nowhere. Any hope of a grand purpose has dribbled away."

Dr. Strange increased his pace as they turned down a bike path. "Well, old directions need new sparks," he declared. "Try connecting to your inner strangeness. Then your direction will no longer matter, since all directions lead to the same place."

Jason's eyes began to tear as they passed the lake. "And what place is that?"

Dr. Strange reached into the pocket of his running shorts, pulled out a handkerchief, and handed it to his sweating patient. "Good. You're feeling sorry for yourself. But tears and self-pity are not the way to salvation."

Jason wiped away his tears. "Easy for you to say. At least you're being paid."

"Drop your hostility, my lad. Anger, rage, and frustration are fine for 'known' folks, those who focus only on facts. But remember, you aren't like them. Your way must be different."

The alarm in the doctor's left running pocket rang. He pulled it out and looked. "Time's up," he sighed. "Back to the office. We'll pick it up again next Wednesday."

That day they stopped for a red light at Thirty-eighth, trotted past the pigeons feeding near the statue of Columbus at the Circle, and again entered the park.

Jason slowed. "I run so slowly," he complained. "Yesterday, on a local street in New Jersey, I tried picking up my pace. I tried running as fast as I could. I panted, pushed, and gave it my all. As I passed a Jehovah's Witness on the street, she smiled, held up her bible, and cheerily said, 'Have a nice walk.' Can you imagine how I felt?"

"Is that your question for the day?"

"Yes. How can I run faster?"

"You can run faster by going slower. Truth is, the slower you go, the faster you go. Here's how it works. When you start to run, you move as slowly as you can until you reach bottom, a place where it feels like you're hardly moving at all. That, in micro-running parlance, is called the *transformation spot*, the mysterious place where slow meets fast.

Silence followed. They passed a maple tree. "At that point, although you're practically flying, it feels like you're hardly moving. And vice versa."

Dr. Strange stopped to tie his shoe. "It's all the same. Slow is fast, fast is slow. Knowing this is a lifetime challenge. It's why we're running together today."

Jason asked, "Is there a technique to this practice?"

"Yes. Here's where your lesson begins."

The doctor slowed to a pre-warm-up jog.

"Good! I can't wait to hear it." Jason, getting excited, surged ahead.

The doctor shouted as he almost disappeared down the path, "That's your *problem*! You're going too *fast*. Slow *down*."

Jason stopped.

The doctor caught up. "Here, do this with me." Strange jogged very slowly, almost in place. In the next five minutes, he hardly moved five feet. "The principles of micro-running are biblical: 'The last shall be first.' In order to win this race, you must come in behind me."

"That sounds very strange."

"Of *course*. That's why we're *here*."

Jason tried it. After losing to the good doctor fourteen times in a row, he gave up. "I can't do this," he said. "Slow is too hard."

"Complain, complain," said the doctor. "Always complaining. Just like your first session. Coming in last is as easy as coming in first. Only it takes practice and a different mind-set."

JASON'S SESSIONS WITH DR. STRANGE CONTINUED over the decade, meeting weekly or monthly. When Jason's business moved to China, they carried on for three years with phone sessions, and Jason ran through Beijing with buds in his ears.

Over time, he also met other Strange patients, all of whom had benefitted from the doctor's unique healing methods and philosophy,

Eventually, the doctor decided to expand his practice by starting the group therapy Strange Running Club. Meeting once a week in midtown Manhattan, they all ended with a run in Central Park.

Time passed. Strange planned the future of his practice. Working together with a New York real estate magnate, he acquired a tract of land with good Westchester running fields and hills in Rye, New York. One year later they broke ground for Fun and Ecstasy Village: A Strange Running Permanent Retirement Community.

Soon most of his former patients moved in.

Jason did too.

His lessons with Dr. Strange continued. He pursued his disciplines, perfecting his micro-running technique, blending slow and fast, and increased his struggle to be last.

Finally, after eighty-two years, at the age of one hundred and two, he beat the good doctor in the annual Over-One Hundred Birthday Celebration run.

Fourteen former patients also participated.

"The younger ones always beat me," Dr. Strange complained.

"Complain, complain," said Jason. "Always complaining."

Then they all went out for a beer.